Wednesday
Walks
&
Wags

The Sunday Potluck Club series

The Sunday Potluck Club
Wednesday Walks & Wags

You can also read Melissa Storm in
Home Sweet Home

Wednesday Walks & Wags

Melissa Storm

KENSINGTON BOOKS
www.kensingtonbooks.com

KENSINGTON BOOKS are published by

Kensington Publishing Corp.
119 West 40th Street
New York, NY 10018

All Kensington titles, imprints, and distributed lines are available at special quantity discounts for bulk purchases for sales promotion, premiums, fundraising, educational, or institutional use.

Special book excerpts or customized printings can also be created to fit specific needs. For details, write or phone the office of the Kensington Sales Manager: Kensington Publishing Corp., 119 West 40th Street, New York, NY 10018. Attn. Sales Department. Phone: 1-800-221-2647.

Kensington and the K logo Reg. U.S. Pat. & TM Off.

ISBN-13: 978-1-4967-2667-4 (ebook)
ISBN-10: 1-4967-2667-7 (ebook)
Kensington Electronic Edition: September 2020

ISBN-13: 978-1-4967-2666-7
ISBN-10: 1-4967-2666-9
First Kensington Trade Paperback Printing: September 2020

10 9 8 7 6 5 4 3 2 1

Printed in the United States of America

To Falcon—
My one, my only, my always love

Chapter 1

Bridget Moore hesitated over the last of her boxes, letting her fingertips hover less than an inch from the taped-up flaps. Might it be better to leave the offensive cardboard container sealed up tight and pushed into the back of her closet where she could forget about it all over again?

That was the thing about moving.

You packed up your life into a series of boxes and prayed they would fit in well where you were going next. Sometimes once-precious belongings needed to be tossed, donated, or passed on to a friend, and sometimes the things you most wished to part with clung to the edges of your life like pesky, persistent burrs.

Bridget's hands shook as she brought them closer to the box, then let them fall to her side. She moved to the window that overlooked the courtyard and stared down at the yellow-green grass. Spring breakup had ended, and now Alaska's warm season was on its way in. The world around her became greener with each day. If the apartment brochure could be trusted, soon the space would fill out with a cascade of beautiful blooms in almost every color of the rainbow.

She watched as a man jogged through the space with two

energetic huskies in tow. They picked up speed and soon zoomed out of view, but not soon enough. Her own dogs had noticed their neighbors and were now barking in an off-key chorus. Rosco and Baby, the rottie and pit bull mix she'd rescued from the shelter a few months back, both had deep, menacing barks. Meanwhile, Teddy, her Pomeranian, had a high, grating bark that sounded at random intervals throughout the day.

Luckily she had found a complex that not only allowed dogs but celebrated them. They even had an after-dinner walking club that allowed neighbors to spend time together and get to know one another, all while giving their apartment-bound canines the exercise they craved. Sure, the place came at a steep cost, but after being evicted from her last residence for illegally bringing pets into the building, she was not taking any chances.

Living here would be a blessing for both her and her canine family, but it did mean that she had to restrict her volunteer work at the shelter to one day per week so that she could pick up more paid shifts at the veterinary office where she worked as a technician while finishing her own DVM degree on the side. She lived on the far Southside of Anchorage, so far that it was almost out of city bounds, so far that it now took fifteen minutes or more to drive to work and to each of her friends' houses.

She knew that the added bit of distance wouldn't change anything with her friends, not when they'd already been through so much together. They'd met more than a year ago at the hospital, of all places. Each was taking care of a parent undergoing chemotherapy. Bridget's mother had been the first diagnosed, but the last to die. Her breast cancer had been in remission for years, so long that her family didn't even think to worry about it anymore.

Until it came back, and that was that.

Oh, her mom had fought hard, and it had been enough . . . the first time.

The second time, the disease had advanced too quickly, and her mother was already weakened by the first battle.

Bridget still missed her every day. Yes, she tried to stay busy so she wouldn't have time to think about how much she missed her mom, but she had so many memories and so many stimuli to trigger them.

That last box of hers was where she tried to keep them stashed away. Notable among the contents were her baby blanket, her mother's engagement ring, and—of course—the scrapbook she and her friends had prepared on the day of her mom's funeral. It gave Bridget comfort to know that they were all nearby but also safely contained.

Her dogs went nuts again, drawing her away from her wandering thoughts. She peered through the window and spotted the man with the huskies returning. The dogs were gorgeous, one black and white and one all white—probably not a husky at all, now that she thought about it. The man had white-blond hair and very pale skin even though he obviously spent time outdoors. Probably took a standing bath in sunscreen before heading outside, she thought with a sad smile.

Bridget herself had never had this problem. Because she was part Inuit on her father's side, her skin turned an alluring shade of light brown after mere minutes in the sun. She often joked that she had two looks—goth girl in the winter, and proud native in the summer. Her dark hair and eyes never altered, but her skin could change so much from season to season that she had quickly given up on trying to wear makeup. Better to have tired eyes than a face covered in the wrong color and sporting a clear line of demarcation at her jaw.

Man and dogs disappeared into one of the side stairwells, and Bridget scooped Teddy into her arms to calm him down.

Otherwise the Pomeranian could easily bark for ten more minutes from the pure excitement of spotting another dog.

Jeez. Just how long had she been standing there hesitating over that box?

The sun still hung high in the sky, but that meant nothing this time of year. With the solstice approaching, it wouldn't sink behind the horizon until around ten that night, which meant she'd be up until at least then herself.

Despite having been born and raised in Anchorage, Bridget had never learned to sleep with the sun up. Even with the best sleep mask and blackout curtains her meager budget could buy, her body somehow still felt it wasn't yet time. That's why she had to keep busy.

Her body was too smart, and so, too, was her heart.

In calm moments like this, both cried out to her, demanding the things they most craved.

Feed me mint chocolate chip ice cream, her body demanded.

Open the box, cried her heart.

And this was the exact reason she now carried a little extra weight around her hips and thighs. This change had come about only after her mother's funeral, and at first Bridget didn't even notice the added weight. When she finally realized she couldn't quite zip her jeans any longer, she found she didn't actually care all that much. Better to get a little chubby than to even think of giving up one of the things that made her happiest now.

When given the choice, she always went with the thing that would make her sigh with pleasure rather than sob in agony. And that something was often ice cream.

Okay, enough fretting over the box already.

Bridget set Teddy on the carpet, then sent a group text to her friends: *I'm all moved in. Come over and check the new place out.*

She paused, then added: *Oh, and please bring ice cream.*

As their excited replies began to pour in, Bridget grabbed the box filled with memories and buried it in the back of her closet. She pushed the hangers with her maxi dresses over it to add some coverage and then covered it with a stack of folded blankets for good measure.

She knew it wouldn't be enough to forget the box's presence, but it was enough to get her head back on straight so that she could focus on all the exciting things that came with her move—like new walking paths for her and the dogs, new neighbors, and maybe even new friends.

Chapter 2

Not even half an hour passed before Bridget's three best friends showed up at the door to her new apartment.

"We're here!" Amy sang as her elderly beagle, Darwin, joined in with a spirited howl.

"Little pig, little pig, let us in!" Hazel called in a deep, animated voice, then followed up with a honking laugh.

Her third friend, Nichole, let out an exaggerated sigh but said nothing more. Of course, if she had, Bridget probably wouldn't have heard it over Teddy's excited barking, anyway.

The little dog bounced after her as she raced toward the door and flung it open with a tremendous feeling of relief. "How'd you guys get here so fast?"

"We may have been sitting around waiting for an invitation," Hazel informed her with a playful wink. She was the first to push her way into the apartment, but the others were hot on her heels.

"We'd have come even faster if we hadn't needed to make a pit stop for ice cream." Nichole set a reusable shopping bag down on the table and began lifting out pints of Ben & Jerry's. Another enormous wave of relief swept over Bridget as she spied her favorite, Mint Chocolate Chunk, among the flavors.

Leave it to pragmatic, introverted Nichole to remember the important details in life. She didn't smile often, nor was she free with compliments, but she always showed up when it counted—and with the right flavor of ice cream.

For all her heartache, Bridget also made sure to count her blessings. She had great friends, got along well with the family she had left, and was on her way to finishing college and securing her dream job as a certified veterinarian. Even though things were hard, they could always be so much worse. She needed to remember that.

Why couldn't she remember that?

Why did what should have been a happy housewarming celebration still feel bleak and cold?

It's because you can't live in the moment, her inner voice whispered, and it was right. She kept the past shut firmly in an old cardboard box while doing her best to avoid the present by staying as busy as possible.

Only the future mattered.

Because it would be better.

It has to be.

Bridget's dogs had no trouble finding joy in the here and now. Even though Darwin wasn't the biggest fan of other dogs, Bridget's three practically fell over themselves trying to impress him. Teddy continued to bark and run circles around the chubby old beagle. Baby dropped his front paws to the floor and wagged his tag furiously, and Rosco gave the other dog a quick sniff, then glued himself to Nichole's side with the clear hope that she'd packed some special treats for him, too.

"I brought cookies!" Amy trilled as she revealed a generously sized Tupperware filled to the brim with one of her famous homemade confections. Well, famous among the four friends at least. "I came up with this recipe earlier in the week, and they're already Darwin's favorite thing ever."

The old dog untangled himself from Bridget's hyper Pomeranian and overbearing pit bull mix, then sat himself at Amy's feet, fixing her with a doleful expression.

"Darwin, you're supposed to be on a diet!" Amy scolded, but then opened the container and tossed him a cookie, anyway.

"Are those safe for them?" Nichole asked, always the voice of reason even though she had no dogs of her own. That didn't stop her from researching everything just for the sake of learning something new. It never failed to impress Bridget how her friend knew an extraordinary amount about almost any topic she could think of.

Amy forced one of the treats into Nichole's mouth before the other woman had a chance to argue. "Try it for yourself and see."

Anger crossed her face first, followed quickly by relief and then pleasure. "Are these for dogs or people?"

"Both!" Amy answered proudly. "My own recipe. Safe for dogs but still yummy for people." She cupped her mouth as if she were going to whisper a secret, but then she yelled loudly enough for the next apartment to hear. *"The secret is molasses."*

"I've going to have to pass," Hazel added with a grimace. "I'm here to see Bridget's new place, not to ruin my bridal diet."

"Oh, like you aren't perfect exactly as you are," Nichole said with a grimace of her own.

Hazel smiled and touched her belly for a brief moment. When she noticed Bridget's eyes on her, however, she quickly removed her hand and strode deeper into the apartment.

"Beautiful layout," she said, inspecting each room while the others trailed her. "Need any help with the setup?"

Bridget chuckled at this. "Oh, Hazel, we both know I can't afford your services. I can barely afford this apartment."

Hazel narrowed her eyes. "And we all know my services are always free of charge for my besties."

"I'll think about it," Bridget promised, even though she already knew what her answer would be. While Hazel was a remarkably talented and highly sought-after interior designer, she was also the worst neat freak Bridget had ever met. If she had a hand in putting together Bridget's apartment, Hazel would no doubt expect it to be kept up to her standards.

Bridget had always preferred clutter to cleanliness, even as a small child. It was part of the reason she knew her father and brother Caleb were happy she'd found a place of her own and moved out of the family home. The rest of that reason rested squarely with her rambunctious pack of spoiled dogs.

"Wow, look at that view," Amy cooed from her newly as-sumed spot at the large picture window. She'd always been the peacemaker of their group, and her timing now helped diffuse the growing tension. "It even comes with a cute neighbor guy," she added, blushing furiously.

Nichole and Hazel both raced to her side.

Bridget went a bit more hesitantly.

Sure enough, the blond man she'd seen earlier that day had reappeared. The group watched in silence as he and his two dogs cut across the courtyard and headed for the main street. Once there, they took off at a rapid clip and quickly disappeared from view.

"Hot, healthy, and clearly loves dogs," Amy mused, tick-ing off each trait on her fingers as if making some kind of valid argument here. "If I weren't already head over heels for Trent, I'd race you to him."

Hazel elbowed Bridget in the ribs. "Who knew your new place also came with a new 'boyfriend,' eh?"

"I guess he's cute. Kind of hard to tell from this far away, though." Bridget shrugged. Ever since Amy and Hazel had both found their other halves, they'd jumped headfirst into playing matchmaker for their two unattached friends.

Nichole fought them hard whenever they so much as suggested a man she might be interested in, which left Bridget as the main target for their misguided attempts at making a love connection.

Honestly, the last thing she needed was a romance.

Not when she already had so much work to do on herself and not when she saw firsthand how devastated her father was after losing his lifelong partner. Bridget wasn't sure how much more loss she could handle in her life, but she knew there'd at least be less of it if she avoided taking on anything—*or anyone*—new for as long as she possibly could.

Chapter 3

Bridget's friends stayed for a few hours before obligations to work, family, and other commitments forced them to return home. Bridget herself had a start time of seven the next morning, when she was scheduled to assist her favorite vet with spays and neuters.

This was a new responsibility, and one she was quite excited to add to her growing list of tech duties. While she wasn't quite as gung ho as Nichole when it came to learning, Bridget did love to master new skills. It was one of the best ways to stay busy.

Set big goals and then exceed them.

She'd always been the overachiever in her family. Her dad had remarked more than once that Bridget's commitment to her mother's care was what had kept her alive so long at the end. The problem, of course, was that a higher bar meant a longer way to fall when she wasn't able to reach it as planned.

Recognizing this tendency didn't make it any easier to avoid it. It just gave Bridget more to fixate on. Maybe this realization played a small part in keeping her up that night. She was filled with excitement and nervousness about the big day ahead, even though she knew she was once again playing into the addictive pattern of achieving success and then promptly growing bored of it.

The lack of sleep might have also been because she was still adjusting to her new place. Maybe her bed wasn't set up for maximum feng shui, or Marie Kondo, or whatever interior organization thing everyone was doing these days.

The fatigue that weighed down her limbs now begged her to accept Hazel's help getting this important piece of her life right. Then again, she'd probably be so tired when she returned home from work tonight that she wouldn't even be able to make it to the bedroom before she fell asleep in an exhausted heap outside the door.

Whatever the case, she lay blinking up at the ceiling for hours before sleep finally took her. Of course, Teddy woke her less than three hours later with another exuberant bout of barking.

Bridget groaned and pulled the pillow over her head, which prompted the fuzzy Pomeranian to jump up onto the bed and dig at her side until she sat up with a huff.

"That's it! You're getting crated and covered at night," she threatened even though they both knew she didn't mean it.

Teddy smiled so wide his tongue lolled from the side of his mouth.

"How can a tiny eight-pound ball of fur make so much noise?" she asked, receiving a loving lick in response.

"You're lucky you're so cute," she grumbled, then pushed the covers aside and pulled herself from bed.

Thanks to Teddy's early wake-up call, Bridget had extra time to get herself ready for work, and she needed every additional minute. By the time she'd downed her third cup of coffee and applied a second coat of concealer to cover the deep purple bruises beneath her eyes, she felt about 75 percent human and only 25 percent sleep-deprived zombie.

Progress.

★ ★ ★

"Good morning," the receptionist called brightly from her place behind the giant circular desk. Two of the office cats flanked her, clearly happy for the company.

"Sheryl. Oreo. Mr. Jinx," she said, greeting each of them in turn.

The cats ignored her completely, having decided they no longer liked her much after she'd adopted her three rescue dogs. Never mind that she was the one who most often cleaned their litter boxes.

"Oh, Bridget. You're here!" Her favorite vet, Dr. Kate Llewelyn, appeared from the back room and came to place a concerned hand on her shoulder. "Rough night?"

Apparently the extra coat of concealer hadn't helped as much as she'd hoped. She put on her best smile, even though she hated hearing what essentially amounted to an observation that she looked like crap. "Just busy with the move," she answered sweetly.

"Ready to do our part to curtail the pet overpopulation crisis?" Dr. Kate asked, lifting her hand from Bridget's shoulder and using it to pantomime the snipping of scissors. "Or do you need some more coffee first?"

"Ready."

"Good, because Napoleon is ready and waiting. C'mon."

Bridget and Dr. Kate worked side by side throughout the morning, mostly keeping quiet as they each gave their all to the animal patients before them. As the tech, it was Bridget's job to cart the animals back and forth from their kennels and the surgical room and to hand Dr. Kate the tools she needed. The exciting new task became second nature by the time they finished that morning's surgeries.

"See?" Dr. Kate said brightly, pulling off her latex gloves and shoving them in the waste bin. "You're a pro already."

Bridget smiled at this. She loved helping animals and especially loved that not a thing had gone wrong with any of their patients that morning. She continued to smile as she floated out into the main waiting area of the clinic to grab a snack from the mini fridge kept at reception.

That was when she saw him for the fourth time in less than twenty-four hours. Her mysterious jogging neighbor.

"Hey," she called before she could stop herself.

He turned his full gaze toward her, his sky-blue eyes attempting to identify her but apparently coming up blank.

"I think we're neighbors," she explained, pushing a hand toward him. This caused the husky at his side to growl defensively.

She immediately pulled away, not afraid but knowing better than to mess with a distressed dog. "Oh, sorry. I didn't mean to upset him. I was just saying I think I saw you the other night going for run. Hey, don't you have another dog, too?"

He stared at her without speaking for a few beats before finally nodding and wiping his palm on the side of his pants. "I'm Wesley. And this is Beau. My other dog is Snow, and it probably *was* us you saw. We try to get out and run at least twice a day, if we can. Dusty Peak Apartments, right?"

"That's the place." Bridget accepted his hand when it was offered again. This time Beau remained quiet at his side.

"I don't think I've seen you before. You must be new," Wesley said thoughtfully. It looked as if he was still trying to figure her out, and that made her a bit nervous.

"Very new," she mumbled, keeping her eyes on Beau as she spoke. "Just moved in yesterday."

"Well, welcome. If you ever want to go for a run, you can find us in 106." Even as he said the kind words, his face remained neutral at best, giving her the distinct impression that he didn't mean a single one of them.

"Thanks. It's nice to know someone there now." Her smile lingered for lack of any idea what to say next.

Wesley turned away and cleared his throat. "I, um, don't have a lot of time. Couldn't get the boss to give me more than an hour for my break. Is the doctor ready to see us yet?"

"Yes, sorry. I'll go get her." Bridget shook her head but still felt fuzzy and vaguely confused by the encounter.

By the time she returned with Dr. Kate at her side, Wesley and Beau had already been settled into one of the exam rooms.

So now she knew one of the neighbors, but she hadn't the slightest idea whether he liked her. Maybe he was just shy, or maybe he was weird with everyone. Maybe Bridget reminded him of someone he'd once known.

Not that it mattered. Not really.

Bridget didn't plan on making any new friends, and she always preferred life when it went to plan.

Chapter 4

Bridget returned home to torn cardboard scattered from one end of the apartment to the other. All three dogs came running to greet her at the door. Her rottweiler Rosco clutched a torn-up box corner between his teeth and wagged his stub in a happy blur. Her pets had never been this destructive at her father's house, where she'd stayed after she was kicked out of her last apartment. But he'd also forced her to keep them confined to her room whenever she left home.

Like her, they just needed some time to adjust.

At least she hoped that was the case for all of their sakes.

Being rescues, both of her larger dogs came with some behavioral issues—chief among them, separation anxiety—as evidenced by that evening's messy display.

After petting them each hello, she grabbed one of the few undamaged boxes that remained and set to picking up the scraps. The dogs followed her while she worked, hoping she'd change her mind about cleaning up and would start a game of fetch or tug instead.

At least she'd already unpacked everything she'd brought with her. She didn't need the leftover boxes, anyway. If they'd kept her dogs entertained during her long shift that day, then all the better.

But what might they destroy tomorrow?

There wasn't anything that couldn't be replaced, except . . .

Her heart sped to a crazy gallop the moment the horrible thought crossed her mind. Her legs jerked to life and carried her quickly across the apartment. What had she been thinking, leaving the bedroom open all day?

Falling to the floor, she grabbed her mother's box from the back corner of the closet. Relief surged through her at once. She'd been so stupid. What would she have done if it wasn't there? If she'd forever lost the last of her mother's things?

Thankfully, both the box and its contents had survived the cardboard massacre. To be safe, she hoisted the precious yet dreaded package to the top shelf of her closet, where she knew no dog could ever reach it. Unfortunately, because of the sloped ceiling of the room, she was now unable to close the closet door, and that meant she'd have to see the wretched thing every time she came to or from her bedroom.

Maybe she could sneak it back into her dad's house or convince one of the girls to take it off her hands for a while.

But then she'd have to talk about it, and talking was the last thing she wanted to do. She'd had more than enough time to cope with her mother's death, known it was coming for years. They'd shared heartfelt goodbyes and even worked on a bucket list together. They'd worked about a third of the way through the items on the list before her mother became too sick to continue.

The partially completed list was in that box, too. Forever frozen between their last completed item (Count the stars) and the one that came after it (Complete a charity race). In fact, they'd already registered for their race and raised funds, but then they had to cancel when her mother became too weak to leave the house.

Bridget had begged and pleaded for her mom to join her in a wheelchair, but she'd flat-out refused. Instead she'd closed the notebook where they'd recorded so many of their adventures together and told her daughter that they'd finished as much as they could in the time God had given her.

And that was it.

She died less than two weeks later.

Bridget pictured that long-neglected notebook now. They hadn't even made it halfway through the list. As much as she hated leaving things undone, she couldn't bring herself to continue the journey alone.

She couldn't even open the stupid box, for crying out loud!

And now she was crying.

Again.

When did the hurt finally go away? Did it ever? Or did it remain such a constant presence that it eventually became a part of who you were? Would the sense of loss one day identify her just as much as her dark hair or her chubby cheeks?

Teddy came over and let out a low whine as he studied his distraught human.

"I'm okay," she told him with a sniff. "I'm okay."

The little dog, appearing content with this answer, licked Bridget's hand once, twice, and kept licking until she finally pulled it away. As soon as she did, Teddy's body went completely still. His ears twitched, and then he unleashed another torrent of excited barks.

Her family had adopted Teddy about seven years ago. She'd been in tenth grade then, and she'd insisted on the adorable dog that looked so much like a stuffed toy that one of its most popular looks had been dubbed the "teddy bear cut." Her mother had also fallen in love with the little fluffball on sight, and that was that. Nobody stopped to research the breed traits, to learn that they'd just brought into their lives one of the noisiest creatures that ever existed.

She'd grown used to Teddy's barking. After all, he did it for everything—joy, pain, alarm, frustration, hunger, *everything*. Her dad and brothers, however, were constantly set on edge by the Pomeranian's vocalizations, even now. That was part of the reason why she'd taken him with her once she was approved for the new dog-friendly apartment.

And she was glad she had.

Teddy had loved her mother, too. He knew what she'd lost, that she'd lost some important part of herself in the process. He knew, but he still loved her with an unyielding ferocity that no human being would ever be able to replicate.

Thank God for Pomeranians.

Drying her eyes with the palms of her hands, Bridget got up from the floor and went to stand at the window to see what had set Teddy off this time. She peeked out just in time to spot her new neighbor Wesley and his dogs crossing the courtyard below.

"Hey!" she cried, tapping on the glass to get his attention. "Hey! Wait for me!"

Wesley paused and waved; an uncertain expression flitted across his otherwise drawn features.

"C'mon, Teddy," she called, shoving her feet into her best pair of sneakers and grabbing the Pomeranian's leash from the hook by the door.

Once again, she wasn't thinking.

Just doing.

Something about her new neighbor intrigued her. Definitely not his winning personality, but . . . something. Perhaps she'd figure out what that thing was after tonight's walk—or at least learn enough not to be curious anymore. She doubted he'd spared her a second thought after that morning's run-in at the vet, and that made him the perfect walking buddy, the very non-buddyness of him.

Both Rosco and Baby tried to follow them out of the apartment, but she didn't want to make Wesley and his two energetic huskies wait a moment longer than necessary. Besides, she still had trouble controlling all three dogs at once, especially given that two of them were stronger than she was.

"I'll walk you when I get back," Bridget promised, blowing each of them kisses, then hurried downstairs to join Wesley, Beau, and Snow on their evening walk. Even if they didn't know it, they'd saved her from the dangerous whirlpool of grief that had been gathering strength, ready to pull her under.

She could not afford to be drowned by her bitter emotions.

Not today.

Not again.

Chapter 5

Bridget hadn't been certain Wesley would wait for her, but when she reached the courtyard a minute later, she found him standing with his arms crossed and one white-blond eyebrow lifted in her direction. Wesley's dogs—Beau and Snow—sat placidly on either side, while Teddy strained against the leash so hard he could scarcely breathe.

He made quite a picture standing with his two large arctic dogs, looking every bit the arctic prince himself. In fact, his hair was so fair, it appeared to blend into his equally pale skin despite its length, which reached almost to his cheekbones. His chin and nose both had a sharpness to them that reminded her of an elegant bird—maybe a swan.

Where Bridget was made of soft curves from head to toe, Wesley had been composed of one angle after another. Even if his unwelcoming expression didn't keep people at a distance, his generally icy air would most definitely do the trick. Never had she met someone quite so unapproachable, which was perhaps why she insisted on seeking him out tonight.

Or maybe she was just a glutton for punishment.

"I didn't take you for a runner," he noted with a smirk,

making her think her latter conclusion was probably the right one.

Bridget put a hand on her hip and scowled. "Should I be insulted?"

Wesley shook his head and worked to hide the small smile that played at his lips. "You surprised me in a good way."

"You invited me because you didn't think I'd come," she said aloud just as the realization struck her. Well, that was a jerk move on his part. Now she was glad she'd stopped him on his way through the courtyard.

"Maybe." He stood straighter and cleared his throat. "But now that you're here, let's go."

Without waiting even a second more, Wesley picked up speed. He and his dogs moved with a practiced fluidity that appeared more like a graceful dance than a sweaty exercise regimen.

"Ready, Teddy?" she asked the little fluffball at her side, wishing she'd had the time or the foresight to change into something other than jeans for her first run . . . well, ever.

She'd been one of the girls who refused to sprint the presidential mile in middle school, preferring to walk and talk with her friends at her normal pace. But now she found herself running after Wesley, her breath already coming out in labored puffs as they rounded the first block.

"C'mon," he called effortlessly over his shoulder. "If you want to jog together, then you've got to be able to keep up."

Is this just jogging?

She'd never moved so fast in all her life. At least not on purpose.

Bridget's heart pounded in her ears. The longer they journeyed on, the more her legs felt like limp noodles attached to bear traps—her limbs had begun to lose all feeling while her ankles screamed in protest.

She wanted to ask Wesley to slow down, but she couldn't get the words out over her gasps for breath.

Teddy—the blessed little munchkin—didn't complain or slow her down in the slightest. If anything, Bridget felt as if she were the one letting him down. Perhaps her father or brother had run him regularly when he was still living at home with them. They were both far more fit than Bridget had ever been. She'd always been the brainy one, the one who joined after-school academic clubs instead of trying out for sports.

Why had she decided to join Wesley again? Oh, that's right. She had absolutely no reason whatsoever.

Once again her impulsiveness had landed her in thick soup. But no, she could reason this out, find a way for it to make a bit more sense.

Now that Bridget thought about it, she had a good job and was well on her way to an even better one, just as soon as she finished her DVM coursework. So perhaps that meant it was time to invest a bit more in her health . . . and her subconscious had figured that out before she did, right?

Of course, she was young still—twenty-three—and had inherited a speedy metabolism from her mother's side of the family, but could she really expect that to last forever? Then again, would getting a bit fat really be the worst thing in the world? She already had chubby cheeks and had recently taken on a somewhat pear-shaped body, and while she considered herself decent-enough looking, she'd never been the kind of girl who needed a boyfriend to feel complete.

"You doing okay?" Wesley called from ahead of her.

"*Oh . . . kay!*" she managed to cry out between fast, desperate breaths.

Her thoughts fell away, taking too much energy to maintain as their run—or jog or *whatever*—continued on well past her point of comfort. Bridget focused her gaze on Wesley's sneakered feet as each hit the payment, then rose in the air once again, propelling him even farther, even faster.

One, two.

One, two.

It became a meditation, drowning out all other thoughts or rationalizations until the only thing she could do was count Wesley's footfalls and keep pushing herself forward in an inexplicable need to keep up with the new neighbor she wasn't even sure she liked all that much.

She could have turned around and taken Teddy home at any point, but she wanted to see this through. For some reason, she wanted to prove to Wesley and that knowing smirk of his that she could do this, that she could surprise him in a good way yet again.

One, two.

One, two.

A few more counts . . .

And then, just like that, they found themselves in the apartment courtyard again.

"Good job," Wesley said as he completed a quick series of stretches.

Bridget fell forward with her hands on her knees, unsure whether she would throw up or simply get high on the sudden rush of oxygen into her lungs. She stayed like that until her breaths became a bit steadier. Her legs, too.

When Bridget finally looked back up, Wesley and his dogs had disappeared. Without saying goodbye.

Chapter 6

Bridget slept much better that night. Of course, every time she inadvertently kicked or stretched, pain shot though her no-longer-jellied legs. She briefly allowed herself to wonder what had happened to Wesley and why he had disappeared so abruptly without saying goodbye, but she was honestly too tired to care much about it—or him.

The exhaustion spread through her body like a calming drug, leaving her too tired to move, to think, to feel anything other than the exhaustion from that night's run.

And she loved it.

So when five-thirty rolled around the next evening, she was dressed and waiting in the courtyard with Baby and Rosco tied to a joint lead.

If Wesley was surprised to see her there, he didn't show it in the slightest. "How many dogs do you have in there?" he asked, glancing toward her third-floor window.

"Just the three," she said, then took off running before he could beat her to it.

Wesley let out some kind of grunt-laugh hybrid as he fell into stride behind Bridget. "I thought you had your fill yesterday," he teased without adding even the slightest hint of a smile.

"You thought wrong," she shot back, picking up speed despite the unhappy protest that had already settled into her previously unpracticed muscles.

He shook his head and muttered something to himself, but Bridget didn't care to ask him to repeat it. She wasn't here for him. She was here for herself and for her dogs. Whether or not Wesley liked or respected her was beside the point, really.

The run went by faster that evening. Even though it hurt even more than the day before, she could already breathe easier. It was amazing how fast progress became evident with this new hobby of hers.

She both loved and hated it at the same time, and apparently that was just the combination she needed to obsess over it. And that new infatuation was perfect for pushing grief out of her mind—at least for the duration of the run.

Once again, her legs screamed for relief, but today she found the pain exhilarating rather than irritating. That pain served as proof she'd pushed herself hard, that she could overcome challenges, that she *would* overcome them.

Running wasn't the first hobby Bridget would have chosen for herself. Actually, it fell a lot closer to the end of her hypothetical hobby list than the beginning. Regardless, though, she'd happened into it, and she couldn't stop now.

That just wasn't how she was wired.

She also wasn't wired to let things go.

"Why'd you leave without saying goodbye yesterday?" she demanded of Wesley when they returned to the courtyard and he started moving into his cooldown routine. *Oops.* So much for not caring about what he thought of her.

"Did I?" he asked, kicking one leg behind himself and then grabbing his foot to deepen the stretch. He didn't even look at Bridget, but rather toward the yellowing grass below.

"Yes," she said, trying to imitate one of his stretches as she stared him straight in the eye. Eventually, he'd look toward her again, and she'd be ready with a heated glare that rivaled his icy indifference. "And you know it."

"Are you planning on running with me every night now?" Wesley shifted his gaze toward her but didn't react to the expression he found waiting for him.

Did this guy have no emotions at all? Or just when it came to Bridget? Whatever the case, his lack of reaction bothered her. How could he *nothing* her when he hardly knew her? The jerk.

"Is that not allowed?" she hissed. "When you gave me that invite, I thought you meant it."

He sighed and dug his fingers into the thick fur of his all-white dog. Bridget recognized Snow as a malamute now, an enormous one at that. She wondered if Snow had a past life as a wheel dog for the Iditarod. He certainly looked strong enough, and he was much better behaved than her own hyperactive canines. That fact also irritated her. So what if her dogs weren't the best trained? They *were* the best loved, and that's what really counted.

Wesley looked at his dog as he spoke. "Look, Bridget. Right? We can run together, but I'm not really looking to make friends here."

"If you don't want friends, then why did you even invite me to join you?" She grew short of breath again, but this time from outrage rather than exercise. True, she didn't want to make friends, either—but that wasn't something you just told people. At least she was trying to be polite. Why couldn't Wesley offer her the same small courtesy?

Wesley shrugged and continued to focus on Snow as he stroked the dog's thick double coat. "I don't know. It seemed like the neighborly thing to do, and you kind of caught me off guard there."

"Me? You're the one who came into my work," she reminded him. "If you don't want me to run with you, just say so."

Wesley shook his head as he looked up at her. "Fine. I don't want you to run with me. At least not if you're going to keep trying to have heartfelt talks at the end of each one."

Seriously? They'd only run together twice, and she'd barely spoken to him either time.

"Heartfelt? Are you kidding me?" Bridget knew she should throw her hands up and walk away, but something kept her rooted to the spot. She shouldn't let him get to her, especially when he could barely look at her, let alone speak to her with even a hint of kindness.

Wesley cleared his throat, but before he could speak again, Bridget launched into a tirade as all the stress she'd kept at bay with that night's exercise therapy came tearing out of her in a jagged burst.

"Don't worry. I'm not some desperate girl begging for a friend. I already have the three best friends in the whole world, so why would I chase after some wishy-washy, lying jerk?" There, she'd given him what he deserved. Now it was time to move on.

His eyes rose to meet hers, the usual sky blue of his iris almost aqua now. It softened his entire face, but it was also too late. "I didn't mean to—"

"But you did," Bridget spat. "Don't worry. I won't bother you anymore." She wasn't sure whether Wesley wanted to respond, but she spun on her heel and marched away with her chin held high in the air.

Chapter 7

That night Bridget found herself every bit as exhausted as the day before but far less at peace. Her mind refused to let her get the rest her body needed.

Rude, arrogant . . .

Wesley didn't even know her, not really. How dare he decide he didn't want to be her friend, or assume she wanted to be his?

Jerk.

As she tossed and turned in bed, his once-enticing features recast themselves in her mind. His pretty sky-blue eyes now appeared sickly, empty. His strong legs were no replacement for a kind personality—definitely not a trade worth making. His smirk now seemed cruel, as if he considered himself above her.

Although she finally managed a few hours of unbroken sleep, thoughts of Wesley continued to haunt her almost immediately upon waking. And during the day, she glanced over her shoulder constantly during her work shift, terrified he might appear.

Wesley obviously hadn't spared the most fleeting of thoughts for Bridget, so why couldn't she get him out of her brain?

Who cared what he thought?
Okay, she did.
But why?

Once Bridget returned home, her three dogs arranged themselves by the door and stared longingly at the leashes that hung nearby.

"Sorry, boys. Not today," she said, shaking her head.

But they refused to lose hope, especially when Teddy heard Wesley and his dogs pass through the courtyard a short while later.

"No, not today!" she shouted, immediately hating herself for losing her temper. Hadn't she chosen this new home because of its dog friendliness?

Friendly dogs. Terrible people.

Well, at least the one person she'd met had turned out pretty awful.

Then again, why should she let Wesley dictate what she could or couldn't do? She'd never been a shrinking violet, and she refused to turn into one now.

"Okay, Teddy. It's your turn today," she told the ecstatic Pomeranian as she laced up her running shoes. "Let's go."

Wesley was nowhere to be seen, but just to be sure, Bridget took a new route around the neighborhood.

Today's internal chant was *I on-ly need me.* Each syllable landed with one of her own footfalls. Wesley had inadvertently shown her a new hobby she had already begun to love, and now, well, she didn't need him for anything else.

I only need me.

She'd once needed her mom but couldn't rely on her now that she was gone. Her dad had become little more than a walking ghost, and her friends all had losses of their own to contend with.

That left Bridget alone.

And that was fine.

It had to be.

Despite her best attempts, everything she'd been running from caught up with her and weighed heavily on her already tired body and heart.

"I on-ly need me," she puffed aloud, her voice cracking on that last word. Why couldn't that be true? She so needed it to be true.

Realizing she hadn't made it very far at all, she turned around and retraced her steps. By some ill stroke of luck, Wesley stood in the courtyard performing his stretches when she returned. Bridget tried to run past him, lest he see her patchy face and red-rimmed eyes.

But then something stopped her and made her turn back around.

He already stood gaping at her; he'd watched her run past without a word. But she still had plenty of words to say to him.

"What you did really sucked," she told him in hardly more than a whisper, feeling more defeated than angry right about then.

"I know," he said with a frown. Finally, an emotion, but it came too late to satisfy her.

"You don't know me at all. I happen to be an excellent friend, but if you prefer to play the tortured hero or whatever it is you're doing, that's fine by me, too. I'm new to running and I need a partner. We don't have to like each other. We don't even have to talk. Just please . . ."

She let her words fall away when Wesley pinched the bridge of his nose and sucked in a deep breath—not out of anger, but perhaps sadness. She hated that she needed him, but his presence gave her something to focus on. Today she'd been eaten alive by her own mind mosquitos.

"It's not about you." Wesley raised his eyes to meet hers. They glowed with that same aqua color she'd seen the night before. "It's about me. And even though that's the oldest line in the book, it's true in this case. You don't want a friend like me."

That last statement caught her off guard. What was he hiding?

Actually, it didn't matter. Whatever his secrets, they didn't impact his ability to run alongside her, to help quiet her brain for a little less than an hour each night. After all, she had secret hurts, too—and she definitely did not intend to share them with Wesley.

"Fine. I won't ask you any questions. I won't ask you anything. Only please can we just keep running together?" she continued, almost begging now. "I need this."

"I know what you mean," he said, finally chancing a smile. That small gesture transformed his entire face. The angles became gentler, more like art than weaponry. She'd never met anyone who looked as he did—or acted like him, either. What made him different? And why couldn't she turn away?

Wesley had been rude, condescending, aloof from the start, yet something about his cold presence soothed her overworked brain, her broken heart.

"I've never had a running partner before. Well, except for these two guys right here." He placed a hand on each dog's head, and they looked to their human friend with lolling tongues and loving eyes.

"If they're both boys, then why did you name them after a Disney princess and a hair accessory?" Even though Bridget had just promised not to ask any questions, she couldn't stop herself from speaking the thought the moment it crossed her mind.

"What?" he asked with a snort. "You can't honestly think that."

She picked up her Pomeranian and clutched the little dog to her chest. "He's Teddy, because he looks like a teddy bear.

Cuddles like one, too. Now how did your two get their names?"

He studied her for a few seconds as if waiting for Bridget to retract her question. When it became clear that she would not, he licked his lips and looked at the black and white dog to his right. "Beau's a rescue, and he came with his name. Short for Beauregard."

"And Snow?" she prompted, nodding her head toward the dog at the left. "He's obviously named for Snow White."

"I've had him from puppyhood. It's part of a . . ." Wesley winced and looked away. "Never mind, that doesn't matter."

Bridget watched as he began to disappear behind his icy shield. Not again.

"And you named him after your favorite Disney princess?" she joked, hoping it would be enough to bring him back into the sun.

Wesley let out a sarcastic chuckle. "Jon Snow, actually. He's my lovable little dire wolf."

She petted each dog, then held up Teddy so Wesley could officially say hello. "Now that we've all been properly introduced, can we do this? Can we keep running together?"

"I'm pretty sure you don't need my permission." Wesley shook his head and sighed.

But Bridget only smiled. "Yeah, but maybe I want it, anyway."

They stood, each waiting for the other to back down. They stood for so long that the dogs began to whine nervously.

Finally, Wesley gave her a quick half smile and said, "Okay, see you tomorrow."

Chapter 8

Bridget and Wesley ran in comfortable silence every evening that week and the one that followed it, too. And with each run, Bridget's legs ached a little less, her breathing came a little easier.

While she found the progress exhilarating, it also meant that she had an easier time keeping up an internal monologue while engaging in what was supposed to be her escape.

"What do you do when it starts getting too easy?" she asked Wesley one day as they approached the end of their route.

"You're not there yet." He smiled and shook his head, both of which he did much more often now that they had started to grow comfortable with each other. Comfortable, but not friendly. Just the way each of them liked it.

"I think I am. I mean, I can talk now." She paused to take a deep breath. "And think, too."

He slowed so that Bridget could fall into step beside him. "Is thinking a bad thing?"

"Sometimes."

Wesley nodded but remained quiet until they reached the courtyard once more.

When they were already partway through their post-run stretches, he spoke again. "You can never run away from what's in your own head," he offered cryptically. "Although sometimes I think it's worth trying."

And with that, he and his dogs retreated to their apartment, leaving Bridget alone with the same thoughts she'd been hoping to escape. More than seven months had passed since she'd buried her mother. Why was the grief still so fresh and new?

She'd hurled herself into one project after the next in a desperate attempt to keep herself busy—and like running, they all worked at first. Then the newness would wear off and her pain would surge again, a tidal wave that had only gained strength from its temporary damming.

In another few months, she'd resume her college studies. She'd already signed up for the maximum course credits allowed. College would keep her busy, especially since she planned to receive perfect grades. But would it distract her long enough to finally forget what she had lost?

Bridget doubted it. Still, she could only keep hoping, keep trying, because the alternative . . .

Life required hope, and in that way, success was oddly counterproductive for Bridget. Achieving the object of her desire would also remove it as a coping mechanism. And what then?

Independence Day passed rather uneventfully with a simple barbecue at her father's. Caleb insisted on playing the role of grill master, but proceeded to burn everything he touched. In the end, they filled up on seedless watermelon and potato chips. While their first holiday without her mother had proved to be every bit as sad as she'd feared, at least it had provided a break in the monotony of what had become her life.

The next day at work further shone a spotlight on all her problems.

She'd almost made it to the end of her shift when Dr. Kate called her in to assist in talking to a distraught pet owner. The fact that she'd chosen Bridget for this task undoubtedly meant the owner and Bridget had something important in common, and Bridget feared she knew exactly what that might be.

Please don't be cancer. Please don't be cancer, Bridget prayed silently as she stepped into the cheerfully painted exam room.

The woman waiting there appeared to be in her late twenties—hardly older than Bridget herself—and her flame-red hair was matched only by the ruddiness of her tear-streaked cheeks. A scared cat hid beneath her chair, shrinking as close to the wall as it could possibly get without disappearing into it.

"This is one of our vet techs, Bridget," Dr. Kate said softly. "Bridget, this is Samantha. We just found out that her cat, Brownie, has late-stage cancer. She's having a really hard time taking the news."

Bridget nodded solemnly; her prayers had gone unanswered for today at least. Apparently, she'd become the cancer expert since the disease had claimed someone special to her. But didn't Dr. Kate understand that it had made her fear the disease that much more?

"I'm so sorry about Brownie," Bridget said, unable to hold back a sniffle. "News like that is never easy."

Samantha twisted a tissue in her hands and glanced up at Bridget. Seeming to see the ally she needed, she asked, "Am I a bad person for wanting to keep him with me as long as possible?"

"Not at all. We all want to keep the people and animals we love close to us for as long as we possibly can." Bridget thought of her mother's box, sealed up tight and buried inside her closet. A constant reminder of what she'd lost. A Pandora's box of grief.

At least she had the box to contain some of her sorrow. Not all the pain had escaped into her world. Not yet.

The woman before her, though, looked as if she might never smile again. "I've had Brownie since I was eight years old. She's turning twenty in just a few months. I knew she couldn't live forever, but I'm also not ready to say goodbye."

Dr. Kate cut in here. "I've suggested that she consider putting him down gently. He's already in a good deal of pain, and it's just going to get worse. Unfortunately, at his advanced age, there's very little chance of his surviving a surgery, and even if he did, it would prolong his life by only months at best."

Why had Dr. Kate forced her into this, especially when her advice was so grim?

Bridget wanted to be a good employee, wanted to second her boss's advice, but she just couldn't. Not when it came to something like this. "I lost my mom about five months ago. She had cancer, too. And you know what? I would give anything for just one more day with her."

Samantha smiled up at her, hope lighting her eyes.

"Can we prescribe a painkiller to help keep Brownie comfortable?" Bridget asked the doctor. Suddenly, it became very important that she not lose Brownie. Even though she could barely see the cat in its hiding spot, she needed to save him, save Samantha the pain of this horrible disease that only took and took and never gave.

It was Samantha who answered. "There is, but I can't afford it. I live paycheck to paycheck as it is and had to eat ramen for a month to even be able to afford this appointment."

"I'll pay for it," Bridget promised without giving it a second thought. Of course, she didn't have any money to spare, either, not with her increased cost of rent and school resuming in the fall. But she could get another credit card or borrow money from her dad or even start a GoFundMe. Anything to give Brownie and Samantha some more time with each other. The way she wished she'd had more time with her mom.

"That would be amazing, but are you sure?" Samantha stopped crying and blinked up at Bridget in hopeful disbelief.

Bridget stooped down and wrapped her arms around the other woman, even more certain now than she had been just a few seconds before. "Positive."

Dr. Kate shook her head in silence, but Samantha's entire demeanor brightened. "Thank you, thank you! You're our guardian angel," she cried, rising from her chair and hurtling herself into Bridget's open arms.

It felt so good to help, even if it was only for a little while, even if it would mean that she, too, would be eating ramen all month. The two of them exchanged phone numbers and promised to stay in touch.

And all the rest of that day, Bridget did feel a little better.

Even though she couldn't help herself, at least she'd found a way to help someone else.

And for now that would have to be enough.

Chapter 9

Brownie was just a cat.

She hadn't even gotten the chance to look at him properly, but that didn't mean Bridget could stop thinking about him—old, overtaken by the world's most hideous disease, one paw in this world and the other in the next.

Dr. Kate had said that Brownie had lived a very full life and for that reason everyone should feel glad. But Bridget refused to feel happy about death, no matter whom it struck. Old, young, healthy, sick . . .

Was it ever the right time to die?

At twenty-three she should be looking forward to finding herself, starting a career, falling in love, not focused on pinching every penny to buy medicine for some stranger's cat, not quaking in fear as she considered her own mortality, as she mourned a mother gone too soon.

The friends she'd made at the cancer ward had lost parents, too, but they were getting better, forming new relationships, moving on. So why then had Bridget gotten stuck?

And would she ever get unstuck?

Honestly, she was afraid to find out.

She grabbed Teddy and cuddled him to her like the plush

toy he'd been named for. She didn't cry, but she also couldn't bring herself to get out of bed and join Wesley for their nightly run.

Helping Samantha with Brownie's medicine had felt good, but learning about the beloved pet's fate had wrecked her. She hadn't even known Samantha before that afternoon, and yet her heart ached as if the woman had been her dearest friend.

The group text she kept with her closest friends, the other three members of the Sunday Potluck Club, chimed, so she fished her phone out and responded with an LOL to Hazel's story about yet another hilarious wedding planning mishap. So far, she'd done a pretty good job convincing her friends that she had moved on, that she was fine.

Earlier that year, they'd all expressed their worry when she threw herself into a massive fundraiser for the animal shelter, vowing to get every cat and dog adopted by Valentine's Day. Amy, Hazel, and Nichole had given generously of their time to help Bridget meet her crazy goal, but they'd all been very clear about how much she'd worried them.

And so she'd gravitated toward other, less obvious obsessions—obsessions she could blame on something other than needing to forget her pain for a few blissful hours. None of them had questioned her newfound joy in running, especially not when she told them she wanted to look and feel her best.

Really, what woman didn't?

And Bridget had lost a few pounds over the past two and a half weeks, but she definitely did not feel her best. If anything, she felt worse than ever, because now that running wasn't effectively emptying her mind, she'd lost one more possibility, one more thing that could have made her feel better at last.

These thoughts played on a disturbing loop as she cuddled Teddy in her darkening bedroom. Sometime later, a soft rapping on her front door triggered Teddy's exuberant barking and forced her from bed.

Had her friends magically figured out that she needed them? Or perhaps one of the neighborhood kids had come around to sell cookies or magazines or something else she didn't need.

Bridget did not expect the person she found on the other side of the door.

"I thought this was you," Wesley said, holding up a bag of takeout with a sympathetic grin.

"What?" she asked, still trying to make sense of why he was here when he'd made it very clear he wanted nothing from her, least of all friendship.

"Your apartment," he explained as he pushed past her into the dining room and set his bag on the table. "I'd only ever seen you in the window, so I had to guess which of these belonged to you. Luckily, I got it right on my first try."

Rosco and Baby flanked him, and he rubbed their blocky heads in greeting.

"But why are you here?" Bridget crossed her arms. True, she could really use a hug, but not from Wesley. Never from Wesley.

"You didn't come running today," he said as if that explained this intrusion perfectly.

She let out an irritated huff. "So?"

"So with the way you were talking last night and then you not showing up today, I worried about you." He smiled again. Twice within the span of a minute. How very unWesley.

"I thought you didn't like me," she reminded him—not really a question, not really a statement, either.

His voice grew louder, firmer. "I never said I didn't like you. I just said I don't want to be friends."

"And not being friends includes bringing me . . ." She peaked into the bag he'd set atop her table and a mouthwatering aroma swirled into the air.

"Some kind of soup?" she guessed once the savory blend had settled into her nostrils.

He smiled for the third charming time and took a step closer. Was he planning to touch or—worse—to hug her? Bridget enjoyed warm, friendly hugs just as much as the next person, but this was not Wesley. Why did he suddenly feel the need to act human around her? Had she really worried him that much?

His next words confirmed that she had. "I didn't know what kind of not feeling well you had, whether you were *sick* sick or heartsick. I figured this would cover both bases."

Bridget sat at the table and pulled the bag toward her, which elicited an immediate sigh of relief from her visitor. "Thank you for the soup," she said as she pulled the container and disposable cutlery from the bag and set it up in front of her on the table. "But I'm getting a lot of mixed signals here. What do you want from me?"

Wesley lowered himself into the chair beside her, his jaw twitching with sudden tension. "I like you, Bridget. You're a good person."

Bridget shrugged off the compliment. She didn't want things to be different between them, didn't need it. "How can you even tell? This is the longest conversation we've ever had with each other."

"I can tell," he answered with yet another smile. This one did something strange to her insides. "Believe me, I can tell."

"So another nonanswer." She let out an exhausted chuckle. "You just might be the most complicated person I've ever met."

Now he laughed, but it sounded sad. "You have no idea."

He sat beside her silently while she enjoyed the hot soup. Normally, she enjoyed conversation with her meals and often found herself carrying on a one-sided talk with her dogs when there were no other people around to engage in lively discussion. With Wesley, though, she felt as if anything she said would be the wrong thing.

Easier just to say nothing at all.

"Come running with me again tomorrow," he said, his bright blue eyes shining with sincerity. "Please."

"Okay," she said, setting her spoon on the overturned lid. "But on one condition."

"Name it." He froze for a moment before easing into a smile. She had yet to decide whether she liked this new smiley version of her normally scowling neighbor.

"No more running in silence. We have to talk to each other." Yes, they didn't have to be friends. They could be colleagues, running colleagues.

Right when it looked as if Wesley would protest, Bridget raised a hand to stop him. "We don't need to talk about our pasts or whatever it is we're running from, but we do need to talk to each other. It will make it easier to forget those things. At least for a little while."

Wesley nodded and held out his palm to shake. "You've got yourself a deal."

Chapter 10

While Wesley's visit did soothe Bridget's anxiety, the next day at work sent it soaring to new heights.

Dr. Kate sat waiting for her in the lobby with a fake smile on her face and a large disposable coffee cup in each hand. She handed one to Bridget, then stood and led her back to one of the private exam rooms—the very same one where they had both met Samantha and Brownie the day before.

"Can we talk about what happened in here yesterday?" she asked, a concerned frown etching fine lines into her forehead.

Bridget wrapped both hands around her latte but found little warmth or comfort. She kept her eyes on her lap rather than raising them to meet her boss's probing gaze. "What else needs to be said?"

"Are you okay?" She craned her neck in an effort to see Bridget's hidden face.

I don't want to talk about it, she wanted to scream. *I don't want a confrontation. Not today. Not ever.*

Instead, Bridget forced a smile, nodded, and took a sip of her coffee. "I'm fine," she insisted, failing to convince even herself.

"Are you, though?" Dr. Kate pressed. "I know it's been hard since you lost your mom, but yesterday with Samantha and Brownie . . ." She sighed and changed tactics, since Bridget flatly refused to take this emotional path with her. "Can you even afford to pay for that medicine?"

"I'll find a way," she mumbled, then clenched her jaw and squared her shoulders. Yes, she'd done something impulsive, but that didn't make it wrong. Bridget refused to feel bad about showing kindness to a stranger in need. "I'm not going back on my word to her."

Dr. Kate ran an index finger along the raised lid of her cup and frowned. "I know you wouldn't do that, but what happens when the next terminally ill pet comes into our office? Are you going to pay for its medicine, too? What about the one after that?"

"I don't know," Bridget mumbled. Dr. Kate was right, of course. She couldn't save them all, no matter how much she wanted to. But did that mean she shouldn't at least try?

"Is this what you still want, Bridget?" Her words came out soft but unrelenting. She wouldn't let the subject go, not until Bridget gave her whatever she was looking for.

"Is what?" Bridget asked innocently. She hoped she'd misunderstood. This woman was not just her boss but her mentor, her friend. Had she given up on Bridget now?

Dr. Kate motioned around the office and sighed. "All of this, this job, this life. It tugs at your heart. Sometimes it hurts. That's the sacrifice you make so that you can help those who aren't beyond saving."

"Are you saying I'm not tough enough?" She didn't want to cry, couldn't cry.

Dr. Kate sighed again. "Bridget, you have such a big heart, but it's fragile, too. I don't want to see this job break you. You're still young, so really think about what you want out of life. You can still change your mind. Nobody will judge you."

She sniffed but held her tears at bay. "Is this your way of firing me?"

"No, of course not. It's just . . ." She stopped and took several long, slow sips of coffee before continuing. "I want what's best for you. It may still be this, and honestly I hope it is. But you need to be honest with yourself, too. Can you promise me you'll think about what I've said?"

Bridget nodded glumly. What else was there to say?

Dr. Kate placed a hand on her shoulder and gave it a squeeze. "I mean, really think about it. This is the rest of your life. You deserve to be happy."

Bridget stood to leave. "Thank you for the coffee," she said, then added after a slight pause, "and the advice. I'll think about it." She could tell that Dr. Kate wanted to hug her, but she drew back. A hug would be admitting weakness, defeat— and Bridget refused to do either.

Her boss took a step away, then nodded as if convincing herself of something rather than Bridget. "Good. Now why don't you take the rest of the day off? Take a long weekend to relax so you can come back recharged and ready to go on Monday."

Bridget was too exhausted to argue.

She needed the money from this job more than ever, but she couldn't very easily handle any more heart-to-hearts with Dr. Kate, either. Where did that leave her? She lived and died with the future, and now suddenly her boss had hinted she might not have one. It was the worst news she could have gotten, because now new parts of her ached, parts that had felt strong and healthy before.

Not anymore.

Her mom had always encouraged her love of animals and her desire to become a veterinarian, and now that her mother was gone, it was more important than ever that Bridget follow through with the dream they'd both shared. Otherwise, how would her mother recognize her from Heaven?

After leaving the clinic, Bridget sat in her car, staring blankly through the windshield as people and animals moved in and out of the building. She didn't want the day off but also knew she couldn't argue with Dr. Kate on the point.

She wanted her routine. Craved it.

Some days it was the only thing that kept her going. She needed something or someone to help her get through the day. Her weekly volunteer shift at the shelter wasn't until tomorrow, and she still had several hours before her nightly run with Wesley. Her father and friends would be at work until at least five that night.

Wait.

Amy didn't work summers, thanks to her career as a second-grade teacher. And being the caretaker of their little friend group, Amy would jump at the chance to help Bridget through this latest setback. Bridget wanted to do it all herself, to throw herself into something that would keep her busy until Dr. Kate forgot her concerns and let her get back to work. . . . But today she needed a friend. She'd never get through the rest of it alone.

Can I come over? Bridget texted without getting into any of the details. Amy didn't need to know them, and Bridget didn't want to give them. She wished the conversation with Dr. Kate had never happened in the first place.

Thankfully, Amy's response was almost instantaneous: *Yeah, of course! See you soon!*

There. Even if her job might not be a constant anymore, at least she knew her friendships were. She, Amy, Nichole, and Hazel had cried together, bled together, survived together.

This bump in the road didn't have to send her veering off course—and it wouldn't.

Chapter 11

The scent of chocolate chip cookies baking in the oven greeted Bridget before Amy could fully open the door to welcome her inside. Funny how her friend's house felt more like home than her own apartment.

"Just another few minutes on the cookies," Amy promised as Bridget bent down to say hello to the animal welcome committee. Darwin wagged his tail slowly and let out that special howl that could only come from a beagle. Amy's cat, Belle, approached slowly and then rubbed her side against Bridget's leg while shaking her tail like a wiggling worm.

Bridget turned awkwardly toward her friend while continuing to lavish pets on the animals. "I only texted like twenty minutes ago. How could you possibly have cookies ready?"

Amy waved off the question with a laugh. "You know me. Baked goods are life."

When Bridget raised herself back to full height, her friend's expression became more tender. "And I know you. Something's wrong. Tell me."

Bridget held her breath as she thought about how much she wanted to reveal, finally settling on, "Rough day at work."

Amy wrapped her in a hug and swayed them both side to

side. "Those are the worst." It looked as if she might ask for more details, but the oven timer saved Bridget from having to find out for sure.

"How's the new place?" Amy asked while using a metal spatula to move half a dozen gooey cookies onto a pair of tea plates. She handed one to Bridget and kept the other for herself. Both women, of course, dug in immediately.

"New place is good. The dogs love it," Bridget answered around a big mouthful of melted chocolate chips and Amy's signature salty-sweet cookie dough. "It doesn't quite feel like home yet, though," she added carefully.

"Have you gotten to know any of the neighbors?" Amy's eyes closed in delight as she started in on her second cookie.

"Just one. We run the dogs together in the evenings."

Her friend's eyes popped open again, a smile crinkling at their corners. "It's that guy we saw from your window. Isn't it?"

"What? How did you know?" Something fluttered in Bridget's chest—the beginnings of an ill-founded crush perhaps, anxiety definitely. She and Wesley had set very clear boundaries on their relationship, and she was fine with that. She didn't need Amy or any of the others complicating it for her. Making her feel things she knew she shouldn't.

Amy pursed her lips into a tight bow and widened her eyes. Her blond eyebrows also rose so high that she took on a cartoonish appearance. An owl, maybe. The kind that knew all the forest creatures by name but still insisted on whoo-whooing ad nauseam. "I think the more important question is, Why didn't you tell us earlier?"

Bridget shrugged. She really didn't want to play this game—not now, not ever. Not only was Wesley all wrong for her, but this was also the absolute wrong time to add any new relationships to her life. Hobbies, yes. People, no. Always no.

"It's only been a few weeks, and our relationship is a bit odd," she tried to explain.

"A few weeks! You've been spending time with that cute guy every day for a few weeks and I had to drag it out of you to find out now?" Amy pushed her plate aside and reached her hands across the table to grasp Bridget's.

Bridget frowned. "It's not like that."

"Plenty of people start off as friends. It doesn't mean you'll stay that way," Amy said with a knowing wink, giving each of Bridget's hands an enthusiastic squeeze.

"No, we're not friends. He was very clear about that."

She let go of Bridget and leaned back in her chair with a troubled pout. "Well, that's weird."

Suddenly, Bridget felt the need to defend Wesley even though a part of her definitely agreed with her friend's assessment. "Actually, it's refreshing. There are no expectations or anything like that. We just enjoy running together."

Amy balked at this. "Uh-huh. So when can we meet him? Oh, you should invite him to come to the Potluck Club this Sunday. I can bring Trent, and Hazel can bring Keith, so he won't be the only guy."

"So it looks like a date, you mean? No way." Bridget shook her head vigorously. This was a bad idea all around.

Suddenly, Amy lightened, taking on her normal easy air and letting all the pressure flit away. "You said you're not friends, but you didn't say that you're not something more."

"We're not."

She let a small smile slip across her face, then called it back almost immediately. "Right. Yeah, of course."

"I'm not bringing him," Bridget insisted, studying her half-eaten plate of cookies.

Perhaps coming here had been a bad idea. Then again, she hadn't known Amy would be in prime matchmaking mode today. Should she have told Amy more about the awful talk with Dr. Kate that morning to avoid being harassed about Wesley? She'd sought out her friend for comfort but instead was given the choice of two topics she preferred not to talk about.

And cookies.

At least there were cookies.

"Maybe not this week, but we'll welcome him in eventually. I just know it." Amy popped to her feet and sauntered back into the kitchen to grab more cookies. It was a wonder she stayed so thin given her giant sweet tooth. If Bridget didn't already love her, she'd probably hate her.

"How could you possibly know that?" Bridget asked, trailing Amy to place her empty plate in the dishwasher. No more cookies for her.

"Friendly intuition." Amy winked again, then thankfully dropped the subject. "Have I told you about the special week I have planned for Olivia later this month?"

"Tell me everything," Bridget said with wide eyes. Finally, a way to escape her problems by focusing on someone else's life for a while. She was really happy for her friend, besides. Not only had Amy started dating a wonderful man, but she'd fallen hard and fast for his eight-year-old daughter. She'd be a great mom someday—probably someday quite soon as a matter of fact.

Bridget wasn't ready to tie her life to someone else's. She simply had too much to do. But she was incredibly happy that her friends had found their perfect matches. For them, it was easier to pass the love they had for their lost parents to a new recipient. For Bridget, that just wasn't the case. And perhaps that was okay.

Chapter 12

After spending a few hours at Amy's, Bridget headed home to spend some quiet time with the dogs before joining Wesley for their nightly run. It also seemed like a good time to catch up on some of the TV shows she'd recorded but hadn't yet had time to watch.

Although she generally preferred browsing through memes and status updates on the web, she was committed to a couple dramas and sitcoms. She'd once enjoyed losing herself in reality TV but kept getting unwanted spoilers when she couldn't keep up with the live broadcasts. With the shows she kept on her to-watch list, she simply needed to catch up with a season before its finale to avoid having important plot twists ruined.

This afternoon, she chose one of her favorite Netflix originals, thinking for the millionth time that she would look terrible in orange. Of course, she got so wrapped up in the story line that she lost track of the hour and had to hurry to meet Wesley in the courtyard . . . five minutes late.

Given what a stickler he was for punctuality, she'd expected him to have started their run without her. Instead, she found him waiting with both dogs sitting obediently at his side as they watched the doorway.

She smiled and waved as she jogged with Teddy to catch up. The way her heart quickened upon catching sight of Wesley made her wonder if Amy's little talk hadn't messed with her mind earlier that day.

Just a little blip. It can't last, she told herself. *I'm happy not to miss out on the run. It has nothing to do with Wesley.*

"Everything okay?" he asked, glancing from her to Teddy as if in search of physical evidence as to why they were late. His white-blond hair fell forward into his eyes as he bent to greet the Pomeranian with a pat and a scratch.

"Sorry we're late," Bridget mumbled, hating the way her body responded to the nearness of his. A little tingle raced through her, and she shivered.

Nope, this was not okay. It also wasn't what she wanted.

Except, maybe it was.

Stupid Amy.

"Let's go," she urged as she pulled Teddy along after her.

Wesley fell into step beside her, and they navigated their route in silence. The whole time Bridget was intensely aware of Wesley and how his body moved. Was she really so weak willed that one little suggestion from a friend could send her headlong into the world's most ill-timed crush?

It wasn't just that she didn't want a relationship; she didn't even want a new *friend*. When they reached the courtyard, she planned to make a quick excuse and then disappear before doing their cooldown stretches. She could tend to those in her apartment or just skip them for the night, since she doubted anything she did could slow the pounding of her heart.

Unfortunately, escape would not be possible, given that her friend Nichole sat waiting on the little bench right in the middle of the courtyard. She raised her hand in greeting and shouted hello.

"She here for you?" Wesley asked with a confused look, his icy eyes boring into hers.

"Yup, that's my friend Nichole," Bridget said with an exasperated sigh. Nichole's sudden arrival couldn't be a coincidence, not when Bridget had just spent the afternoon with meddling Amy.

"Hi, Bridget. Hi, Teddy. Who's this?" Nichole asked with a smirk that suggested she knew exactly who it was and that he was part of the reason for her visit this evening.

"This is my running . . ." Friend? Buddy? Ultimately, she settled on "partner," because it didn't imply they had any connection beyond exercise. Because, really, *they didn't.*

"Wesley," he introduced himself with a nod but no smile. It had taken Bridget many encounters with Wesley to earn one of his rare smiles, so it was only fair that Nichole didn't get one for free.

"Okay, well, see you tomorrow." Bridget turned and motioned for Nichole to follow her up to the apartment.

Teddy barked his head off until Nichole bent down and scooped him into her arms for a tight cuddle.

Bridget gave her friend the leash and then raced up the stairs, thighs sore from tonight's run but not quite burning.

Nichole was several paces behind, and Bridget felt as if she were waiting forever for her friend to catch up. When they were both inside, she shut and locked the door, turning on Nichole for some kind of explanation.

"Amy sent me," Nichole said, confirming her suspicions. "She says you had a hard day but wouldn't open up about it with her. So she sent in the pro."

After greeting Baby and Rosco, Nichole marched to the kitchen and grabbed a yogurt and Diet Coke from Bridget's fridge. "Want anything?" she offered before digging in.

Bridget always found it odd when her friends offered up things that already belonged to her, but it seemed they were just raised differently. "No, I'm okay."

Nichole let out a sarcastic little huff. She was the master of sarcastic little huffs—always had been. "No, you're not. That's why Amy sent me, remember?"

Bridget groaned and sank onto the couch. All three dogs jumped up, each vying for the seat of honor right in the center of her lap, within prime face-licking distance.

"So, are you going to tell me what's wrong, or do I have to dig it out of you?" Nichole asked with a raised eyebrow as she spooned a bite of yogurt and fruit sauce into her mouth.

"Why does it matter so much? And don't you remember the rule we made at the hospital? Each of us is supposed to be able to grieve her own way, no judgment." A third heart-to-heart in the space of a single day? No, thank you. She needed to get Nichole to leave before the last dregs of her patience disappeared.

"One, it matters, because you matter a whole heck of a lot. You know we love you, B, so just accept that and move on."

Nichole swallowed and took a deep breath before continuing. "Speaking of moving on, we've all noticed that your way of grieving is avoidance. It's why the rest of us have healed, and you . . ." Nichole made a wavy gesture with her hand and frowned.

"I *what*?" Bridget demanded. The only thing she hated more than meddling was trailing sentences and implied conversations. If Nichole had something to say, then she could say it and leave.

Nichole's brow pinched in sympathy. "You seem to be backsliding."

Chapter 13

Backsliding. That word stung, largely because Dr. Kate had implied the very same thing earlier that day.

Yes, lately Bridget's life had become hard . . . or, hey, maybe it had always been that way. And apparently everyone saw that things were tough for her at the moment. So then why wouldn't anyone give her a break?

Lots of people in their early twenties had trouble finding themselves. At least Bridget was trying. She hadn't disappeared into addiction or allowed herself to get washed out by an unhealthy, draining relationship. She'd been there when her family and friends needed her; she also worked hard and had a plan for the future.

It could be so much worse.

But then, it could also be so much better.

Bridget shrugged and turned her head away so that Nichole couldn't see the glassiness that had overtaken her eyes. She would not cry, especially not in front of Nichole, who would only try to *help* even more.

"I don't know what you want me to say to that," Bridget muttered. She glanced out the window, looking for something to distract her, calm her, but could see only sky and brick from her position on the couch.

"Say something. Say anything. Let us help you. You don't need to do it all yourself." Nichole had deep, dark circles under her eyes, almost like bruises. Why was she so fixated on Bridget when clearly something was wrong in her life, too?

"Do what?" Bridget tried her best to focus on making this confrontation as short as possible. Maybe if she showed Nichole that her worries were unfounded, the other woman would back off and find some other project to keep her busy during her off-work hours.

"Come to grips with your mom's death. It totally sucks that she's gone, but she's not coming back. You, however . . . *you* need to come back." Nichole's mouth made an exaggerated circle around the word *you*, calling Bridget's attention to her chapped and peeling lips.

Oh, so she was deflecting. Nichole had problems of her own but clearly found it easier to focus on Bridget's. *How fair.*

"I haven't gone anywhere," Bridget mumbled into Baby's silky fur.

She hated confrontation, especially when Nichole was on the other end of it. Her social worker friend saw right through any attempt to rationalize or explain away one's behavior. That made her an annoying adversary. Strange that she'd decided the best way to help Bridget was to start a fight with her, and it would only escalate if Bridget shared her suspicions about Nichole avoiding some kind of personal trauma of her own.

"I agree," Nichole said, surprising Bridget. "You're running and you're running but you're not going anywhere."

"That's called a treadmill," Bridget muttered sarcastically, flashing a lopsided smile. "Lots of people like using one for exercise."

Nichole tossed her yogurt container in the trash and popped

the tab on the can of soda she'd taken for herself earlier. "Not a great way to live life, though, and you know that better than any of us. Also, sarcasm not appreciated. I'm trying to help you here."

"I didn't ask for your help. In fact, if you'll recall, I asked for Amy's when the dogs and I got kicked out of my last apartment, and helping me ended up hurting her."

She hated the way that episode had played out. If Bridget was the busy one, Hazel was the bossy one, and Nichole was the direct one, then Amy had always been the nurturer. It had only been natural for Bridget to seek out Amy's help before turning to the others.

Unfortunately, Amy had a hard time putting herself first— so much so that she hadn't even mentioned there was a problem when Bridget and her rambunctious dogs destroyed her house and almost ruined her fledgling relationship with Trent.

All the more reason for Bridget to just handle her problems herself—or not. Whatever. Everyone had struggles. At least she could identify hers. Avoid them.

Nichole nodded thoughtfully. "I remember that, but it doesn't mean that you were wrong to ask. Amy needed to learn a lesson about saying no, and you need to learn the same lesson for different reasons." She looked so tired; even her hair seemed to fall more limply against her shoulders. Bridget needed to get her back home for Nichole's own good as much as Bridget's.

Still, she couldn't help arguing in her own defense. "That doesn't make any sense. Amy and I are in completely different places."

Nichole scrunched her mouth and scoffed. "Oh, please, Bridget. You may have yourself fooled, but you can't fool me. In case you've forgotten, this is my job. I help people dealing with trauma all day, every day—or at least for eight hours of it. You think I don't see the signs of unresolved grief in my own best friend?"

"I don't know what you see when you look at me, but I never asked to be ambushed with your psychoanalysis." Bridget tried to be patient, compassionate, to understand that this was just the way Nichole did things, but her tolerance for this intervention—or whatever it was meant to be—was wearing thin.

"What are you hiding from?" Nichole pulled out a dining room chair and took a seat, leaning forward with both arms resting on her knees as she studied Bridget.

"I'm not hiding. I'm right here."

"Are you?"

Bridget groaned. "You're really annoying. You know that?"

"I love you. I'm worried about you. We all are." Nichole's tired eyes widened, as if inviting Bridget to look into her soul and to see the sincerity of her words written there.

"I can take care of myself."

"It's not weakness to let those who love you help. Please, please, Bridget, tell me how I can help."

"I just need time." Time her mother never had. That's what it always came back to, wasn't it?

Nichole cocked her head to the side. "Is that all?"

Bridget shrugged. "I think so."

"Okay, but I'm coming again at this same time next week. And every week after, until you'll talk to me about how you're feeling or tell me how I can help. I'm not giving up on you, and I really hope you don't plan on giving up on yourself, either."

Nichole rose from her chair and pulled Bridget up for a hug, but Bridget couldn't help feeling suffocated.

Chapter 14

For Bridget, Saturdays meant a full day volunteering at the animal shelter. Bridget used to spend much more of her week donating time to her favorite cause, but her new, higher rent required more paid hours at the vet to make ends meet—especially now that she was paying for Brownie's pain medicine on top of everything else.

She'd planned and organized an incredible rescue event several months back with the goal of finding every homeless pet a family for Valentine's Day. She'd given it everything she had and then some. In fact, when two applicants pulled out at the last minute, she'd decided to adopt Baby and Rosco rather than leave them as the two remaining pets in the stark, echoing kennels.

Despite all the work she'd put into that event—and the hours of work her friends had put in as well—nearly all the cages and kennels were once again filled with stray and abandoned animals.

It just never stops, she thought as she leashed up several of the smaller dogs for a shared walk. Three of the four had been with them for a few months now, which made Bridget worry they'd have a hard time finding homes going forward. It just wasn't fair. The volunteers and staffers put in so many thankless hours to match each animal with the perfect person, and almost as soon as an animal was out the door, a new pet in need came to fill its place.

"Wait up!" May, one of the few full-time staffers, called from behind Bridget just as she was about to slip outside with her pack of minis.

Bridget tensed but did as asked. May wasn't her favorite person to deal with, even on her best days. After all, May had been the one to volunteer to host a big adoption event for the shelter cats and then dropped the ball so spectacularly, it took Bridget and all her closest friends to pick up the slack. How she'd been promoted to staff after that, Bridget hadn't a clue.

May bent her tall frame to clip a leash onto one of their newer rescues, a German shepherd mix who showed some aggression to smaller dogs—smaller dogs like the four Bridget already had at her side.

She tried to hide the exasperation in her voice as she urged May to leave the shepherd and take one of the joined pairs of littles off Bridget's hands. Seriously, how had this woman worked her way up to one of the few highly coveted staff positions? She couldn't handle even the simplest tasks, yet she made decisions that affected all the people and animals here each and every day.

Bridget waited impatiently as May returned the shepherd mix to its kennel and then finally accepted two of the dogs Bridget had leashed up earlier.

"Nice day, isn't it?" May remarked, glancing up at the fluffy white clouds that dotted the bright sky. And despite the mundane observation, she was right.

Summer in Alaska made up for its winters. Bridget's mother had always joked that was how God kept people here when every accumulated inch of snowfall intensified their desire to flee. Still, May definitely wanted something if she'd resorted to small talk as a way of easing into whatever request was forth-coming.

"Yes, and what can I do for you on this beautiful day?" Bridget asked, forcing a smile. Better just to get it over with. Besides, Bridget didn't want any trouble at the shelter, espe-cially considering she already had issues to deal with at work and with her friends.

May shook her head and laughed; her graying hair blew in the gentle breeze. "You always know what I'm going to ask before I even get a single word out."

That's because you're always asking for something, Bridget men-tally answered. On the outside, she nodded cordially and con-tinued to smile.

May looped the leashes tighter around her hand and cleared her throat. "Anyway, I'm sure I don't need to tell you that we're getting full up again. It just breaks my heart, seeing all these pets without families."

Here it comes…

"And, well, your Date-a-Rescue was such a smashing suc-cess, I wondered if it might be time for another big event so we can clear those cages and make space for more animals who need our help." Despite being taller and thinner than Bridget, May was dragging behind.

Bridget gulped as she adjusted her pace to allow the older woman to catch up. "Yeah, that makes sense." Perhaps if she played dumb, May would get the hint and go to someone else this time—or, God forbid, do the work herself.

May clasped her hands, yanking the fat Chihuahua and long-haired terrier mix back a bit too abruptly when she did. Her face shone with a telling brightness—clearly, she was about to tell Bridget exactly whom she expected to run the entire thing. "So you'll take the lead on this one, too?"

Bridget's eyelids fluttered as she sucked in a deep breath and tried to consider the situation rationally. The animals did need help, and she was the best person to provide it. Especially if her begging off meant that barely competent May would likely wind up in charge.

She glanced down at the two Chihuahuas that pranced merrily along the trail before them, eagerly darting from one side of the path to the other to take in as many new smells as possible. They needed this every day, not just whenever a volunteer made time and remembered to walk them. They needed love, a home, family.

Then again, just last night, Nichole had warned Bridget that she needed to learn to say no sometimes. But how could she look at these sweet, misunderstood dogs and not do everything in her power to give them a better life? How could she say no to any pet in need?

She couldn't.

"I'd be happy to help," she told May, and meant it.

It didn't matter that she didn't know where the extra time would come from or if she was mentally strong enough for another huge charity event or that she worried she'd end up bringing even more animals into her home if every last one was not adopted by outside families.

All that mattered was that she was needed and she'd been given another excuse to avoid her pain by staying busy.

Yes, she would do it.

But this time, instead of dragging her friends down with her, she would do it all by herself.

Chapter 15

The more Bridget thought about it, the firmer her decision not to inform her friends about the massive new task she'd taken on for the shelter. They had all given so much to help her make her deadline on the last one, and she didn't want them to feel obligated to volunteer again.

If she told them, they'd definitely jump to her aid whether or not she asked. They were always babying her because she was the youngest of their group by several years. She needed to prove to them that she could manage her life without any training wheels or safety nets.

So it only made sense for Bridget to handle this on her own.

That night, she was more than ready to pound the pavement in hopes of shaking loose some of her mounting anxiety. Even though she felt confident in her ability to get things done, she knew she'd have to work long hard hours to fit it all in—and she refused to give anything less than her best effort. A run would clear her mind so that she could focus.

When she entered the courtyard with Baby on one side and Rosco on the other, Wesley looked up from tightening his shoelaces with a kind smile. "How did last night go?" he asked, his strong calves flexing as he finished his task and returned to a full standing position.

It took Bridget a second to remember that Nichole had been waiting for her when they'd returned; it took her even longer than that to puzzle over his seemingly friendly interest in her life. What a weird week this had been.

"Oh, Nichole. Yeah, she just wanted to talk." She did a couple of quick stretches as an excuse not to have to make eye contact.

But Wesley closed the distance between them and bent to the side so that they could talk face-to-face. "Did it help?"

"Help with what?" Bridget stretched the other way, and finally Wesley got the hint. She didn't want him close. His nearness made it much harder to ignore the attraction that seemed to grow with each new day. Why was he getting so up close and personal tonight, anyway?

"I don't know." Wesley's voice deepened, his words becoming less melodic as if he were pulling something back, hiding it away. "Whatever you needed help with, I guess."

She shrugged. "Not really. Not the way running does."

Wesley's smile widened when Bridget finished her stretches and turned his way. "Then let's go."

They jogged in silence for a couple blocks, not yet at their full speed. Their first turn was fast approaching. It led to a long stretch of road that gently sloped upward, adding a bit of extra resistance that helped bring Bridget's heart rate into the ideal cardio zone. They always turned off before reaching the steepest part of the incline, though.

"I think we're ready for a longer route," Wesley called to Bridget, who was just a couple steps behind him. "Keep straight."

So no hill at all today? He guided them off-road into a nature park she hadn't realized was so near to the apartment complex. Now instead of smooth pavement, they worked their way over uneven dirt trails and under a gorgeous canopy of bright green trees. The road zigged and zagged rather than offering a straight path, which meant Bridget had to focus more intently.

By the time they finished that night, her muscles burned as they hadn't since her first few times out, but it had all been worth it for that view. The two of them worked on their cooldown routine side by side as the dogs lolled on the grass.

"Sometimes when things start to get to easy, it's time to mix it up. To push yourself harder, because sometimes you surprise yourself by just how much you can handle," Wesley told her before returning to his apartment with both his dogs in tow.

Well, that was weird.

Almost as if he'd been giving her advice about something beyond running. But how could he possibly know the troubles that were plaguing Bridget's heart these days? She hardly admitted them to herself.

Even after a few weeks spent running beside him, Wesley was still a mystery to her. He insisted they weren't friends, yet he paid such close attention to her that she sometimes found herself wondering if he could read her mind. Now he was doling out advice, too?

Why do that if he had no desire to get to know her outside of their shared hobby, a hobby that would be over as soon as the lengthy cold season hit?

He wasn't pushing her the way her friends did, at least not yet. And whenever he said something too personal, he either visibly retreated into himself or turned tail and ran back to the safe solitude of his apartment. The whole thing between them felt crazy, undefined, completely different from all the other parts in her life.

Perhaps that's why she kept going back to him night after night.

Perhaps that's why she longed to know more about her strange, stoic neighbor. If she gave him time, would he continue to open up to her? And was that even what she wanted? She didn't know, but she looked forward to finding out.

Yes, even if it was a bad idea. Sometimes the best parts of life started out as the worst ideas. It was all in what you made of it once you'd committed, and Bridget wanted to see this thing with Wesley—whatever it was—through. At the very least it added a bit of mystery to her life, which had begun to feel far too predictable since her mother's passing.

Nichole was wrong about her.

Bridget wasn't stuck. She was just moving in a different direction than the rest of her friends had chosen, a more scenic one, like tonight's route with Wesley. It might not have been the straightest shot to their destination, but the interesting new terrain and beautiful foliage lining their path had made it well worth the detour.

Chapter 16

Sunday brought the Potluck Club's weekly meeting. This time Nichole was playing host in her clean, sparse condo; her two cats, Salt and Pepper, remained in the bedroom, staring out at the guests through a slight crack in the doorway. Nichole had rescued them from Bridget's shelter after she'd fallen in love with cat-sitting Amy's elderly feline, Belle. Now Hazel was the only one of them who didn't have any pets, but perhaps she and Keith would correct that after they said their *I do*s at the end of the summer. Bridget, for her part, couldn't picture a life without lots and lots of animals in it.

Bridget wasn't normally the first of them to arrive, but this week she made sure that she came a little later than usual, hoping to avoid any awkward alone time with Nichole, should she want to have another prying heart-to-heart. Plus she needed time to plan and prepare a dish that was adequately quirky but also super cheap. Pennies would need to be pinched for a while, and that meant no buying fancy cheeses for a fondue spread or bringing sea urchins or some other bizarre food and forcing everyone to give it a try.

She'd always been the strange and adventurous one in their group, and if that changed now, her friends would only worry more. This felt like a great time to learn a new exotic cuisine, so she settled on North Indian. The biggest expense were the new spices she needed to add to her collection.

Everything else, though? Blessedly cheap.

The helpful clerk at the Asian foods store suggested she make *aloo matar* for her first foray into subcontinent cuisine. This required potatoes, green peas, onions, and tomatoes. And it was pretty easy to make, too, although it took far longer than expected and she might have burned the onions a little. Luckily, that was easily masked with spices and a dollop of plain yogurt. She just hoped her friends would like it.

"Whoa, that smells . . . *flavorful*," Nichole commented when she greeted Bridget at the door.

"Figured I'd take you all on a little culinary adventure today," Bridget answered, lifting the lid on her serving dish without missing a beat. "And just for that comment, I expect you to have a double portion."

Bridget's curry joined Nichole's InstaPot mac and cheese, Amy's strawberry rhubarb pie, and Hazel's meatloaf for quite the eclectic spread that week. They all had such different ideas on what constituted a good meal.

Bridget preferred adventure, while Amy favored sweet comforts. Nichole valued speed and ease above all else, which was why she'd always ordered takeout before she'd found her dream appliance in the InstaPot. Hazel usually stuck to family recipes; they were her way of remembering the good times without lingering on the bad.

"Shouldn't there be rice or naan or something?" Hazel asked now as she scooped some peas and potatoes onto her plate.

Bridget laughed and slapped her forehead. "I forgot to take the rice out of the cooker. Oops."

"That's okay. I'm sure it's plenty good without," Amy said peaceably, then stuck a giant spoonful into her mouth.

Her bright blue eyes were flooded by a sudden onslaught of tears, and her cheeks and forehead were mottled with red. "Holy mama, that's hot," she cried, squealing and fanning herself frantically.

Everyone laughed as Amy drank a full glass of water followed by an entire glass of skim milk from Nichole's fridge. During the ruckus, Hazel pushed her serving to the far edge of her plate. Nichole, at least, tried a few very small bites before calling it quits.

Okay, so maybe Bridget added a little too much spice to compensate for the burnt onions, but it wasn't that bad. Still, she could finish her own portion only by adding half a container of yogurt to counteract the spices.

"Maybe next week we can skip the culinary adventure," Amy suggested with a sweet smile, drawing laughter from all around the table. "I think I like my food considerably *less* adventurous."

"You like everything considerably less adventurous," Bridget reminded her, and all the friends laughed again.

"So what's new with everyone this week?" Hazel asked the group. She pushed her plate to the side and grabbed some lotion from her purse. She applied it practically every hour on the hour as part of her pre-wedding skin care regiment. Seemed like overkill to Bridget, but then again she'd never minded a few rough, patchy spots here and there.

Bridget sent up a silent prayer that Amy and Nichole wouldn't get their fourth friend involved in their new favorite hobby of worrying over Bridget. Amy and Nichole, she could handle. One showed her concern through baking and the other through private talks. Not Hazel, though. She'd jump in to take action and *fix* whatever needed fixing.

The thing was, Bridget wasn't broken, nor had she ever been. She'd worked very hard to keep herself together, and

Hazel's fiddling would, no doubt, make her carefully maintained composure crumble to dust.

Bridget sat quietly, not wanting to offer up the news about her new event-planning assignment for the shelter—and especially not in front of fix-it-all-in-a-jiffy Hazel.

Amy glanced her way and nodded so subtly no one else could have possibly noticed unless they'd been watching for it. "Trent surprised me with an invite to go camping with him and Olivia next weekend. I agreed as long as he promised to get me home in time for my weekly time with my girls."

"The first rule of the Sunday Potluck Club is that you better have a darned good excuse for missing meetings," Bridget recited with a wistful smile. She'd learned this the hard way when she'd chosen to stay in bed to catch up on sleep and Netflix, only to find her three friends at her door with a traveling smorgasbord.

"You? Camping?" Nichole sputtered before breaking into a hearty laugh.

"Hey," Amy objected, tapping her fists on the table gently. Amy did everything gently. "Stranger things have happened!"

Hazel got out of her chair and wrapped an arm around Amy. "I think it's great. I mean, soon we'll have more than just *my* wedding to plan, if you catch my drift."

"Everyone catches your drift, each and every time," Nichole said, rolling her eyes.

Amy turned beet red, which was especially noticeable given her fair features. Blond and light, just like Wesley, Bridget thought with a smile.

No, bad! She needed to stop thinking of him when he wasn't around. She took another big bite of her curry and let the tingling, jabbing spices steal her focus away from the man she wasn't meant to think about.

Chapter 17

Bridget had not been looking forward to returning to work Monday morning. She still didn't know how she'd handle another talk about her future with Dr. Kate. Seriously, why did everyone in her life demand that they have heart-to-hearts all of a sudden?

Maybe that was why she liked Wesley so much lately.

He just let her be. Hazel, too, hadn't been bothering her much, but she'd also been too busy with her wedding planning to really notice that something might be off with Bridget. Once Hazel figured it out, though, she'd be the one to dig in the hardest.

Then there would be no safe place that Bridget could hide, no talking her way out of whatever intervention would surely follow.

Dr. Kate had called one of the other techs to help her in surgery that week, which meant Bridget was off the hook. She'd managed to make it through the entire morning without any run-ins with her well-meaning boss, when a familiar face turned up in the waiting room.

She would never forget those large, shining eyes or the auburn dyed hair that came with them—never, not as long as she lived. Samantha had returned to the animal clinic, and this time without her cat, Brownie.

Bridget's heart fell straight through the floorboards and continued to sink all the way down toward the center of the earth's molten core.

Samantha didn't smile, so she didn't try to force it, either.

"Hi, Samantha," Bridget said softly.

"Hello," the young woman answered, choking on a sob at the end of this short greeting. Her hair had been pulled back into a hasty ponytail, and her shirt looked as if it belonged to part of a pajama set. It had probably taken Samantha everything she had just to get out of bed. Bringing herself all the way to the vet's office had, no doubt, taken real internal strength.

Bridget placed a hand on the woman's shoulder, felt her sobs intensifying, the tremors in her body becoming more and more pronounced.

"Thank you for helping Brownie," Samantha sniffled. "He died last night in his sleep. I wanted you to know."

"Oh, I'm so sorry." Bridget wrapped her arms around Samantha and held tight while Samantha continued to cry. Bridget had become an expert on crying as she watched her friends' sick parents, and then her own mother, die. Everyone in her world had cried so much, she had begun to wonder if it even meant anything anymore, if it wasn't just what their bodies had trained themselves to do.

Samantha grabbed a tissue from her front jeans pocket and blew hard. "Don't be. You made his last days easier. Gave me the chance to say goodbye. He was old, and—"

"Shhh." Bridget hugged her even tighter, eliciting a fresh round of tears from Samantha. Her own body responded in kind, weeping fat, silent tears as it recognized the pain in another. "You don't need to explain anything. Brownie was so lucky to have a long life with a person who loved him so, so much."

Bridget couldn't be sure how long the two of them stood there, each taking silent comfort from the other. It wasn't until Dr. Kate offered Samantha a chilled bottle of water that Bridget even remembered she was still in the vet clinic and not in the oncology ward of the hospital.

Apparently grief had become part of her muscle memory; Samantha's loss had transported her back to that day with her mother. The last day they'd ever have.

Hadn't it been just like this when her mother's light, bubbly spirit had finally left her heavy, diseased body? Everyone had told Bridget how sorry they were for her loss, but they didn't know her mother, didn't know what she'd lost. They'd only known the sick, fatigued shell her mom had become in her final days; they couldn't possibly understand.

And in trying to comfort Samantha now, Bridget was doing the same thing that had only made Bridget feel worse following her own loss. Everyone said, "I'm so sorry" or "My condolences" or "She's in a better place now," but no one knew the person they were so politely mourning. That was the biggest loss of all—that so many people had missed out on getting to know such a beautiful person.

"Tell me about Brownie," Bridget whispered, using what little strength she had to bring a reassuring smile to her face. People always told her she had a beautiful smile, angelic even, and she hoped it would help Samantha now. "I want to hear all your favorite memories. I want to know what he'd do now if he saw you looking so sad."

Samantha sniffed, pulled out of Bridget's arms, and then returned Bridget's smile full force. She became beautiful in that instant, a beacon of pure love.

Bridget couldn't look away as the grieving pet owner told her everything that had endeared Brownie to her over the years.

"He was such an amazing cat. I wish I'd had the chance to get to know him better," Bridget said, when it seemed Samantha had run out of stories to share.

And when Samantha left a short while later, Dr. Kate found Bridget almost immediately. "How did you know just what to say?"

Bridget wrapped her arms around herself for strength. "Because I've been there, too."

Dr. Kate nodded, calling Bridget's attention to the extra rosiness of her cheeks. Had she perhaps been crying, too?

The veterinarian offered a sad smile and placed a shaky hand on Bridget's shoulder. "Maybe I was wrong in what I said last week. Your heart is huge and vulnerable, but that could be the very thing that makes you a great veterinarian."

"Thank you," Bridget sputtered. She hadn't known many authority figures who'd admit they'd judged a situation incorrectly, especially so shortly after it had happened. All Bridget had done was be herself, both when she'd offered to help Samantha and when she'd comforted her after Brownie's passing.

Even though life was sometimes hard, it moved forward, no matter what. Things changed; things got taken away, but things always kept going.

Chapter 18

The rest of Bridget's workday was slow and uneventful following the emotional visit from Samantha. That was probably for the best, considering she had no idea how she'd be able to focus on her job responsibilities.

Her mind kept returning to Brownie.

To her mother.

To the fact she'd hardly been back to visit her father's house since moving out the second time. Those who had died were lost to her. She couldn't change that, but she could do her best not to lose those who remained.

No one in her family had ever been much of a phone person, and her father had flat-out refused to take up texting, so no in-person visits meant no communication at all. And that would just not do.

Guilt gnawed at Bridget the entire drive back to her apartment. After all, her father had sustained just as big a loss as she had. Probably even a bigger one. She'd lost her mother, but he had lost his partner in life.

Needing to do whatever she could to right the situation immediately, she stopped off at her apartment to collect the dogs, then swung through their favorite drive-through to grab a hot meal for them to share. Thank goodness for credit cards, especially those that allowed the user to spend over the limit. There was no way she'd show up empty-handed now after playing the absentee daughter for so long.

Her father greeted her at the door with a huge smile and a weak hug. He'd never been much of a hugger, but Bridget suspected that he had used up all his tolerance for the small gesture of comfort following her mother's funeral. Back then, everyone had latched on to anyone in the family they could find and hung on like a persistent, condolence-spouting burr. They meant well, but that didn't change the fact that their presence had become a nuisance.

"How'd you know I was coming?" Bridget asked her father, noticing that his shirt collar stood up on one side and lay flat on the other. She patted his shoulder as an excuse to tuck in his popped collar.

"It's hard to miss you and the canine crew coming down the street," he answered with a wink and then immediately raised his collar again. "You're right on time. Pizza should be here any minute."

"Actually I brought burgers and fries. Just need to go grab them from the car." She couldn't help but laugh at the vision of her middle-aged father standing there like some frat boy, collar popped and waiting for his pizza to arrive.

He met her chuckle with one of his own. "Then we'll have ourselves a feast tonight."

"Is Caleb home?" Bridget asked, searching the living room for any sign of the encroaching mess that tended to follow her brother wherever he went. Even though he was five years her senior, Caleb had never once moved out of the house. He claimed he'd rather be a starving artist than a corporate drone and had taken up one creative pursuit after the next, only to lose interest the moment it became too hard.

Their eldest brother, Devon, had left home to pursue col-

lege in the lower forty-eight, and they'd seen him only a handful of times since—their mother's funeral having been the latest.
He kept busy as the kind of corporate drone Caleb swore he'd
never become, but then again, Devon had money, a gorgeous
home, and a loving wife, and her other brother had nothing of
note.

"He's at a writing conference this week, so it'll just be you
and me."

Bridget stomped her foot in frustration and said, "Dad,
you didn't pay for it, did you?"

"Well, how else was he going to be able to go?"

"Why does he have to go at all? It's not like he's an actual
writer."

"Hush, none of that. He's really been working hard on his
novel these past several months. I know you don't see it, because to you, he'll always be your screwup big brother, but
he's changed since your mother passed."

"Well, I'll believe it when I see it." She hated how Caleb
manipulated her father—had manipulated both parents when
their mother was still around. She'd lived here for a couple
months between apartments, and all she'd ever seen was her
brother goofing around on the Internet or playing video
games. There was no going to work, no earning a living or re-
paying their father's generosity and patience.

She was just about to apologize when the pizza delivery
truck pulled into the driveway. Although she didn't have much
to spare, Bridget insisted on paying the delivery boy herself.

"I'm sorry I haven't been around more lately," she said as
she set the bright orange box on the table in front of her father. "Things have been really busy with work."

"Oh, I understand. Don't worry about me." His smile
lessened but didn't disappear completely. Maybe he was han-
dling things better than Bridget had assumed. "Let's go eat."

She grabbed some paper plates from the cupboard and filled

two glasses with water from the tap. "What have you been doing to stay busy?" she asked while settling into the spot at the table that had always been hers.

"Caleb and I have taken up bowling. I'm thinking of joining a league." He pretended to pick up an invisible bowling ball and hurl it down the table.

"Dad, that's great!"

He chuckled. "I'm not any good at it, but I do have a good time."

"And work's good?"

"Work's work. It's as good as to be expected." He'd been saving up for an early retirement so that he and her mother could travel in their old age. Instead, a lot of that money had gone to the funeral. Now that he had no urgent reason to retire, he probably wouldn't until management forced him out.

As they ate their doubly greasy meal of burgers and pizza, her father asked all the usual questions about her work and life. Bridget had always been closer with her mother, and now that she was gone, she often had a hard time bridging the distance that had grown between her and her father over the years.

She needed to make more of an effort before it was too late, before God called him home, too.

"How about I come bowling with you and Caleb sometime?" she offered right as she was polishing off a second piece of pizza.

Her father shook his head as he wiped his lips on a thin take-out napkin. "You don't have to do that. I know how busy you are."

"Not too busy for my family," she countered with a stern expression. Even though until now that hadn't exactly been true. "Actually, I've been learning how to make Indian food. Maybe I can bring some over for dinner when Caleb's back from his conference."

"Sounds nice," he agreed, and then they finished the rest of their meal in silence.

If her mother had been there, they'd be laughing and singing and reliving all their favorite memories from over the years. She wondered if her father felt her absence as acutely as Bridget did.

If he wasn't only pretending to be okay.

Just like her.

Chapter 19

Bridget stayed with her father only for a couple hours. Without her brother there to serve as a conversational buffer, the two of them didn't have much of anything to say after the initial hellos and requisite updates. The awkward quiet only served to spotlight the gaping hole right at the heart of their family.

It would be too late to join Wesley for their evening run, but perhaps she could still get a few blocks in to work off the unhealthy dinner she'd just scarfed down with gusto.

All three dogs went crazy with excitement while they climbed the stairs to Bridget's second-floor apartment. They pulled against their leashes so hard that Bridget practically face-planted on her way up. Usually, this level of enthusiasm was reserved for when they were on the *other* side of the door, waiting for someone new to enter.

Rounding the hallway corner, she finally spotted the reason for their intense joy. Wesley stood with one shoulder against the wall as he waited outside her apartment door. Instead of his usual uniform of work-out shorts and a T-shirt, he wore a pair of faded jeans and a fitted navy-blue polo shirt. The dark coloring of his outfit highlighted his fair features rather than washing them out, the blue of his shirt bringing out the bright tones in his eyes.

He shoved his phone into his pocket and pushed off the wall, an enormous smile making him appear more handsome than ever before.

"Hey," Bridget said casually. She hated to admit it, but she liked seeing him here. But why show up at her apartment and wait around all night when he had no idea where she'd gone or when she'd be back? Yes, she'd skipped their running session that night, but she'd had to beg and plead to even be included in the first place.

Had something changed between them to encourage him to wait for her? To make her happy that he had?

"Hey," Wesley replied, his eyes searching hers as she approached, his open smile now replaced with a furrowed brow and puckered frown. "You didn't come down tonight. Is everything okay?"

He'd worried about her? Was that because her absence had thrown off his routine or because he'd actually begun to care?

She handed him the dog leashes so she could focus on unlocking the door. "Everything's fine. Just paid a visit to my dad."

His face fell. "Oh. Why didn't you tell me you wouldn't be coming?"

"It was a last-minute decision, and we haven't exactly exchanged numbers." Bridget kept her words casual, light, even though she desperately wanted to ask him why he was here and find out where they stood.

"Then we should do that now." He handed her his unlocked phone and waited, rocking slightly between the balls and heels of his feet. "It's weird running without you now. You're like my lucky sidekick."

She laughed at this. "Lucky for what? And why are we exchanging numbers all of a sudden? I thought you didn't actually want me running with you, and I thought we weren't friends."

Wesley shifted his eyes to the floor and rubbed the back of his neck. When he looked up again, a ruddy blush had consumed half his face. "I thought that, too, but I guess I was wrong."

"About which part?" She couldn't help biting her lip as she waited.

"Both." He didn't offer anything else, only a deeper, more intense blush as he raised his eyes to meet hers. There was a question somewhere in those soft baby blues, but Bridget was too distracted by the fluttering in her chest to figure out what it might be.

She eyed him suspiciously, then sighed and motioned for him to join her inside the apartment. "You really keep a woman guessing. You know that, Wesley . . . ? Uh, I don't even know your last name. I also don't know what you do for work, or really anything beyond the fact that you have two dogs and you like to run."

That's it. Focus on the facts. No need to get lost in his eyes, especially since you don't know what secrets they may be hiding. You know next to nothing about him, and he doesn't know you, either. Not really. Not in any of the ways that matter.

Wesley stepped into the apartment and hovered near the doorway rather than entering fully. Bridget wondered if he might also be giving himself an internal warning—or pep talk. She also wondered what he hoped to accomplish here. What was his end goal?

He waited for her to unleash and settle the dogs, then licked his lips and said, "I'm Wesley Wright. And running and dogs are the most important things about me. But if it's so important for you to know, I'm a short-order cook at Bailey's."

Bailey's was one of her favorite restaurants in the city. The atmosphere was homey rather than fancy, and the food didn't cost much but tasted great. She hadn't been in a while and would definitely have to change that situation when she had a bit of extra cash to spare. "Bailey's? I love that place. Have you been working there long?"

"Not long, no." Wesley shook his head as he leaned back against the wall. Why did it constantly feel like one step forward, three steps back with him? He was the one who'd sought her out. He was the one who had said he wanted to be friends now. Then why was he still being so cagey about sharing himself with her?

Bridget decided that the best way to find out would be to ask him directly, even if it made them both uncomfortable. "Why do you suddenly want to be my friend, Wesley Wright?"

"Because I worried about you when you didn't show up tonight, worried in a way that implies maybe we already are." That made sense. He didn't want to care for her but had accidentally started doing so, anyway. She could definitely understand that, since the same thing had happened for her.

She smiled, hoping it would put him at ease and help him open up to her a bit more. "And if I agree to be your buddy, you'll stop worrying?"

He chuckled, although his eyes remained serious, unblinking. "Don't let me force you into anything."

Bridget rolled her eyes and then pointed toward her couch. "Have a seat. If we're going to be friends, then I need to know a lot more about you."

Chapter 20

Bridget pulled one of the hard wooden chairs from the dining room and set it across from the couch. She had only the one sofa and would rather face Wesley while talking to him than sit beside him. Of course, all three dogs piled on the couch with Wesley, choosing comfort over loyalty.

"Traitors," she murmured as her guest laughed and lavished attention on each of them. Teddy in particular appeared to believe he was in the presence of royalty. His bright pink tongue lolled from the side of his mouth, and he panted and snarfled so heavily, Bridget had to wonder if he was literally choking on the excitement of having Wesley in their home.

"They're good dogs," he said, bending forward to give Teddy a little kiss between the ears—and just like that, any remaining doubt Bridget had about whether the two of them could actually find a way to become something to each other disappeared.

If animals were Bridget's life, then that aging fluff of a Pomeranian was her heart, and Wesley had instantly charmed her. Wesley also seemed more at ease now that he was flanked by canine supporters.

She laughed, not because anything was funny but simply

because it was the only way to smile even bigger. "Until now, they've always seen you when we're about to go for a run. It's no wonder you're their new favorite person."

"Or maybe they just think I'm a good guy," he said, lifting his soft eyes to meet Bridget's. They changed colors, she realized. Wesley's eyes were always blue, but the exact hue changed with his moods—light and happy, bright and wanting, dark and stormy. *Fascinating.*

She uncrossed and recrossed her legs, then met his inviting gaze head-on. "Well, get on with it," she demanded, the silence feeling more intimate than any words possibly could.

Normally she fell into friendships naturally, easily. This situation with Wesley was anything but. They'd started with arguments and false invitations, grew closer over time, and now had announced they'd like to start an official friendship.

Who did that? Only Wesley, apparently.

He lifted his head a bit higher and asked, "With what?"

"Your life story," she answered with a wry smile. It seemed he didn't know how to proceed, either. At least they were well matched.

He chuckled. "There's not much to tell. I'd much rather hear about you."

She shook her head. "Nope, not falling for that. When a guy only wants to talk about you, it's because he's hiding something about himself."

"But we're not on a date. We're trying to become friends here," he reminded her. Trying? Earlier, he'd said they already were. Also there was no way a date could be any more uncomfortable than this.

"And friends share, so dish."

Wesley laughed again, presumably at her assertiveness, while Bridget felt heat rise to her cheeks at the mention of dating. Except for a brief boy-crazy period in high school, she'd tended to prefer friends to boyfriends. Friends made fewer demands on her time. Friends didn't try to change or mold her to better fit into their already established lives.

She liked Wesley, yes. Found him handsome, even. But that didn't mean she'd try shoving such a big new piece onto her already overflowing plate.

Besides, it would be nice to have a friend nearby in case she ever needed a cup of sugar or something, right?

"Tell you what," Wesley said with a sudden trace of a frown. She wondered why that might be, since their conversation had been so lighthearted until now. Awkward but light. Kind of like her. "We'll take turns. And I'll even start. Good?"

Bridget shrugged and motioned for him to go ahead. She focused on his hands as he continued to lavish affection on her dogs. They accepted him, and she trusted their judgment. Not that they'd ever shown any sign of disliking anyone, but they were extra fond of Wesley and that had to mean something.

When she met his eyes again, he cleared his throat and shared another fact about his life. "Okay, so I was born and raised in Homer. Only moved to Anchorage fairly recently."

"What brought you here?"

He lifted a finger and wagged it at her. "That's not what we agreed to. I shared a fact about me. Now you share one about you."

She took a deep breath. Why did this feel like a game of truth or dare? She'd always chosen dare when growing up, but today's game was composed exclusively of truths. No questions, though. Only a fair exchange of facts.

"My dad was in the army, so I was born out of state, but we've been in Anchorage for pretty much as long as I can remember. My parents—I mean, my dad—still lives in the same house where I grew up."

Wesley caught her small slipup but didn't ask any follow-up questions. Was this because he was a stickler for the rules he'd set for this interaction, or because he figured she'd share if she wanted to?

Now it was his turn. "I went to college for engineering but never got to finish. Now I'm a cook instead, and honestly I think I like it way better than I would have liked being an engineer."

She nodded. Despite his seriousness, she couldn't picture him as an engineer, either. When he'd told her about working at Bailey's, his entire face had glowed with pride and excitement— as if he was exactly where he needed to be and doing what he was meant to do. She wondered if she had the same glow about her when she was at the vet clinic, hoped she did.

"I'm going to school to be a veterinarian. I had to take a year off to help my mom when she got sick. She died at the beginning of this year, and I've missed her every single day since."

Wesley tensed, sitting straighter on the couch, his hands growing still on the dogs' backs. "I lost someone close to me, though not in the same way. It's hard, but it does get easier with time."

"Thanks," she said, meeting his eyes again and offering a sad smile. "I hope you're right, because I don't think I can live with this giant gaping hole in my chest much longer."

Wesley stood and untangled himself from the pile of dogs, then approached Bridget's chair and kneeled. He took both of her hands in his and squeezed. "It gets easier. Running helps. So do friends."

Friends would help.

And now thanks to Wesley, she had one more.

Chapter 21

Nichole came by again later that week just as she had promised—or more accurately, threatened. She even brought her InstaPot so the two of them could make dinner while they chatted.

"Sometimes it's easier to open up about the hard things when we have a mundane physical task to distract us," she explained as they moved into the kitchen. "So, here . . . chop the onions."

"The onions, really?" The onions were a big part of what had ruined her latest cooking adventure, and she still felt a bit sore about it.

If Nichole realized this, she did nothing to indicate it. Instead, she smiled and pushed a large Vidalia onion into Bridget's chest. "Yup. That way if you need to cry, you can blame it on them. No one will ever know otherwise."

Bridget scoffed at this. "I'm not going to cry. Sorry to disappoint you." She tossed the onion from hand to hand until Nichole caught it midthrow and set it down on the counter.

"I don't need you to cry," she said, grabbing the cutting board from its place on top of the fridge and placing it before

Bridget. "Just be honest with me and yourself," she continued as she retrieved a knife from the chopping block.

"I'm always honest." Bridget peeled the skin from the onion and set it aside.

"Good. Then this will be a breeze." Nichole plugged in her InstaPot, then turned to Bridget while she washed her hands in the kitchen sink. Her demeanor visibly changed as she took off her friend hat and donned the social worker one. Nichole had always been a bit more serious and severe than the others, and now she set her jaw and narrowed her eyes.

"Today we're going to take stock of your life as it currently is. Next week, we'll focus on how you'd ideally like your life to be, and then decide on a list of actionable items to help you bridge the gap between the two."

"I feel as if I should be handing you my insurance card right now, Dr. Peterson. Do we really need to be so clinical about this?" Even though it was hard to share her worries with her friends, it was even worse to think she required professional help just to get through life—especially since she was perfectly fine. Just a little sad was all.

"You like busywork, and I like doing things right the first time, so yes." Nichole positioned the can opener over a can of kidney beans and began to crank. "So let's start talking about the things that take up the most space in your day. You finish those onions, then slice these tomatoes, and I'll take notes for us to refer to later."

"But . . ." Bridget's argument fell away when she saw Nichole fish a small notebook and pen from her purse and set them on the counter.

Once back, Nichole dumped the beans into the pot and began fiddling with the ground turkey. "If you're not sure where to start, just walk me through a typical day, and I'll take notes on things we should talk more about."

Bridget nodded and wiped away the beginnings of a tear. "Stupid onions," she muttered.

"That's okay, let it all out," Nichole joked. It felt weird, though, since Nichole had never been one to fool around, especially when in social worker mode. She seemed to be trying extra hard to get through to Bridget, which was equal parts touching and irritating.

Clearly, Nichole wasn't going to just drop it, which meant the faster Bridget went through this exercise, the faster it would all be over. "Well, I work at the vet five days a week. Volunteer at the shelter one day a week. There's Potluck Club on Sundays, and I run each night now with Wesley."

Nichole grabbed her pen and jotted everything down. "What else takes up your time?"

Bridget swiped at another tear with the edge of her shirt. "Wasn't that enough?"

"For a normal person, yes. For you, not really. Keep going."

"I'm returning to college in the fall. That'll be a big thing. But that's pretty much it." Bridget chopped quickly and a bit clumsily, anything to get this interrogation over with as fast as possible.

Nichole wiggled her pen between her fingers. "So you're telling me that out of twenty-four hours in a day, you are always"—she dropped her eyes to the notepad and read—"at work, school, volunteering, running with Wesley, or at Potluck Club with us?"

"No, of course not. I sleep, too. And eat. And drive from place to place."

Nichole bobbed her head again, starting a second column on the paper to list these activities, too. "How about TV? Reading? Chores?"

"I do all that, too. Though maybe not as much as I'd like."

Nichole raised one eyebrow as if she expected whatever she said next would have a big impact. "How about family?"

"I saw my dad last night. I do need to visit him more. Caleb was out of town. You know where my mom is."

Her friend grimaced.

And Bridget was quick to apologize. "Sorry, this whole thing makes me a little uncomfortable."

"Why? Let's unpack that." Nichole's eyes narrowed again; a small smile played at the corners of her mouth. She loved solving the mysteries of the human heart and had just landed on a new case to investigate.

"I don't know. I guess I'd rather just deal with this stuff on my own."

She raised an eyebrow and smiled more widely. "Yeah. And how's that working out for you?"

Bridget finished with an onion and dumped the discarded bits into the trash. "You're annoying. You know that?"

Nichole's expression remained serious, her pen poised over the pad. "Yes, I do, but I'm okay with you being mad at me, if it helps you in the long run."

Bridget sighed. Why did Nichole make it so hard to stay mad at her? "Why are you so sure I need help?"

"Because running isn't just a fun new hobby you've taken up. I know you, and I know how you process things."

"How do I process things?"

Now Nichole was the one to sigh. "Well, this wasn't how I pictured this activity going, but fine. You deal with negative feelings by throwing yourself into any and every new activity, hobby, or project you can find. The more upset you are, the more you take on, trying to drown out your feelings, but that only works for so long. Doesn't it?"

Chapter 22

May accosted Bridget the second she walked into the shelter for her Saturday volunteer shift. "There you are! I've been waiting all week to hear about what you have planned for our next big adoption event and how soon we can put it on. Do you think the first weekend of August would work?"

Shoot. Bridget hadn't even begun planning yet, and yet somehow she needed to have everything ready in just three weeks?

She hung her head, ashamed. Although May was far too pushy, ultimately the dogs and cats were the ones who would suffer if Bridget delayed too much. "I had to clear a few other things from my schedule this past week so that I'll be able to really dig in and focus once I get started. I'll have my proposal ready to share with you and the board when I come in next week, though."

May clapped her hands and beamed at Bridget proudly as if already taking credit for whatever great ideas she might present. "Perfect. So should I tell them we're a go for that first weekend in August?"

"Um . . ." How could she ask for more time without appearing incompetent? But, then again, how could she not ask for more when this had all just been sprung on her last week?

"Great. It really helps to have a date nailed down." May didn't seem to have a worry in the world. Well, of course she didn't, since she would hardly lift a finger to help with any of the planning or administration.

"No problem," Bridget answered, even though it was actually a huge problem. She loved the shelter, loved the animals there, but could definitely do without this particular person in her life.

That night, she told Wesley all about the shelter, their Date-a-Rescue event last Valentine's Day, and the fact that she needed to put together a new one fast. She kept her feelings about May to herself, though.

They kept up a constant stream of chatter during their runs together now, and Bridget found that she enjoyed it even more than simply focusing on his footfalls and her heartbeats. Despite an awkward start, he'd become the one person to whom she most enjoyed telling about her day—probably because he had no expectations of her and she had none of him. That made things so much easier.

"Whoa," Wesley said, summing up the situation perfectly in just that one word. "All that seems like a lot to handle in such a short span of time. Is this May person helping you put the fundraiser together once you come up with the plan?"

"She thinks she is, but nothing she does is ever actually helpful. And it's not a fundraiser so much as an adoption event." Okay, so maybe she would share her May rage just a little bit. It felt good to express her unhappiness, as if by stating it aloud her problems became lighter, less daunting.

"Well, maybe it should be. I mean, you said the part that took so much time before was putting together all the adoption profiles and date cards. What if instead of doing all that work again with this new batch of animals, you focused on raising awareness and funds?"

Hmm. She liked that, provided May would go for it. "What were you thinking?"

"Get people to the shelter. Get them talking about it. Do something fun that people will enjoy taking part in even if they're not looking to add a new pet to the family."

"Like a silent auction?" she asked, warming to the idea even more.

"Yeah, or a charity race." Wesley lifted his knees higher as he ran to animate his point.

Bridget groaned, but it quickly turned into a breathy laugh. "People do those all the time."

"Yeah, and I bet it's because they work."

"My mom and I were supposed to participate in one. It was the next thing on our bucket list before she . . ."

"Got it," Wesley said when her words trailed away.

Bridget pumped her legs faster, pulling ahead. She needed the extra burn in her muscles to take the focus off the fissure in her heart.

Wesley caught up easily and pulled to her side, never an easy task considering their canine running mates. "You need to do this," he said. "For your mom."

"It was her bucket list, not mine." Bridget focused on the outline of the mountains on the horizon. She would not cry, and she would not unload all her grief on Wesley, either. She just needed to get through this run, this shelter event, this summer . . .

But Wesley kept pressing. "You said 'our,' like the bucket list meant something to both of you. Whether that was on purpose or not, it seems like maybe you need to finish it to help give you closure."

"Closure on what? My mom dying?" A part of her had

liked it better when they talked less. She was so very tired of people speculating about her emotions, thinking they knew what was best for her when she'd already figured it out for herself.

Wesley frowned. "I don't know. Only you know that."

"Now you sound like my friend Nichole."

"Is that the one who ambushed us last week? She seemed nice."

"That was her, and my friends are nice. Just pushy." She turned to him and tilted her head to show that she now included him under this annoying umbrella, too.

Apparently, he took this as a good thing, which was definitely not the way she'd intended it. "I guess that means it's okay if I push you a little, too, seeing as we're friends now and all that."

"Remind me to never invite you to Potluck Club."

He laughed. "To what?"

Shoot, shoot, shoot. Why had she said that aloud? "It's just a thing we do every Sunday. We each bring a dish and check in on one another and catch up on our lives. It used to be a support group, but it's kind of moved past that."

"Sounds like a great thing to have in your life."

Did she have to invite him now that she'd brought it up? The others would tease her mercilessly, not that they weren't already but . . .

Wesley laughed again, but this time it put her at ease. "I can see the gears in your brain turning. Don't worry, I'm not looking for an invite. But maybe I can help you with the cooking. Sundays, right? What are you planning to bring tomorrow?"

Now this was a topic she could talk about at length without feeling embarrassed or overwhelmed. "I've been learning Indian cooking. Last week's *aloo matar* was a miss, but I have high hopes for this week's *biryani.*"

"Let's make it together," he suggested. "I think I have the ingredients for curry, too, if you want to remake last week's dish to figure out where you went wrong."

Where she went wrong. . . . If only it were that easy to fix life.

Didn't work the first time?

Just try a second time. Easy.

Only it was anything but.

Chapter 23

The next morning, Bridget stood outside Wesley's first-floor apartment with an overloaded bag of ingredients in one hand and her favorite glass serving dish in the other. "Knock, knock!" she called, finding it too difficult to maneuver her load to attempt an actual physical knock.

Wesley's two arctic dogs, Snow and Beau, let out frantic, high-pitched howls and slammed their bodies against the other side of the door in their eagerness to say hello. Honestly, she preferred her gang's chorus of deep, throaty barks over the earsplitting howls assaulting her ears now.

The door opened, but Wesley stood facing the other way, his hand lifted in a command to the dogs, who now sat silently, tails thumping against the hardwood floor. "Come in," he said and moved to the side, keeping his stare firmly on the dogs.

Bridget stepped inside and made her way straight to the kitchen. She'd expected Wesley's apartment to follow the same blueprint as her own, but the two spaces looked nothing alike. Where hers was spacious and comfy, Wesley's was small and cramped with cold hardwood floors. Still, the place was immaculately kept, with sparse furnishings and an even sparser gathering of personal items. The walls were white, the cabinets white, the blinds white, the floors light honey. It was as if she'd stepped inside a giant egg.

"Good boys," Wesley said, releasing his dogs from their command with a fast click of his tongue.

"How long did you say you've lived here again?" Bridget asked as he wandered over to join her. Her place already appeared a hundred times more lived in even though she'd moved in only recently.

Wesley stretched both arms overhead, luxuriating in the space that Bridget found far too small. "Almost a year now."

"I didn't know you were a neat freak. I might not have agreed to be your friend if I had," she joked. Not a single belonging was out of place. Everything had a spot, most of it tucked away out of view. Bridget would go crazy without her homey clutter; it was what made a house a home as far as she was concerned.

Wesley just shrugged, completely unbothered by the gentle criticism. "I like keeping things tidy. Makes small places seem lots bigger. Don't you think?"

"Yeah, sure thing. But, um, is there enough room for us both in here?" Like the rest of his apartment, the kitchen had to be half the size of Bridget's—at most. The only available counter space stretched out about three square feet beside the sink. The oven swung out on the other side of the tiny L that flanked the room. It, too, had a small swatch of counter to the side, but the microwave took up the entire space. The end result was a cramped triangular area that hardly fit one person within its boundaries, never mind two.

Wesley pulled open a drawer and withdrew two wooden cutting boards. "We'll do prep at the table. C'mon."

Bridget took a seat at his equally diminutive table. Two semicircle laminate flaps folded out on either side, but the room didn't boast quite enough space to open them up. No wonder

Wesley ran his dogs so much. The three of them must be trip-ping over one another all the time in this place.

Bridget glanced around in search of the husky and mala-mute and found them lounging by the front door happily.

"Seems vet techs make more than short-order cooks," he said with a simple smile as he handed her a French knife and two tomatoes. "Don't worry, though. I have all the space I need."

She watched as Wesley returned to the kitchen and gath-ered onions, garlic, and little green peppers. He sat down op-posite her and picked up a sleek and shiny knife. "The initial prep work for both dishes is pretty similar, so we're going to make them both at the same time. Walk me through what you did last time you cooked Indian."

"Well, I didn't have any of those," she said, nudging one of the small peppers with her index finger.

"Green chilis are essential for good curry," he explained, slicing one in half to show Bridget the seeds inside. "If you use canned or frozen ingredients, it makes the end result a little less special. I'd rather have the most delicious meal possible than save a few minutes of prep time."

Bridget nodded. "Well, I used canned tomatoes, canned peas, and red chili powder, so I probably did a pretty mediocre job last time around."

Wesley's eyes widened at her horror. "Please tell me you at least had fresh potatoes."

"Yup," she announced, happy she'd done one thing right.

"Which spices did you use?" Wesley asked, moving on to the garlic.

"Curry powder, red chili, salt, and coriander."

"Oh, yeah, we can do way better than that. For starters, you want turmeric for color. Freshly grated ginger adds a bit of zing to the mix. And fresh is best for coriander, too."

"I don't think I've ever seen fresh coriander." She tilted her head to the side as she thought back to the sand-colored powder she'd purchased from the grocery store last week.

"I bet you have." Wesley chuckled for a moment before stopping abruptly and gaping at her with his jaw slightly askew. "Wait, you're not one of those people who swears cilantro tastes like soap, are you?"

"I love cilantro," she said, fighting off a craving for her favorite shrimp tacos. *Maybe next week.*

"Good, because I wouldn't have accepted any other answer." He laughed all the way now. "Cilantro is the leaf of the plant. Coriander is the stem."

"Which do we use?" Bridget asked, waiting while Wesley moved back to the kitchen and extracted a thick bunch of the plant in question.

"Both, if you'd like. One during the cooking process and one as a garnish," he told her after rinsing the leaves in the sink.

"Okay, let's do it."

Time passed quickly as they worked together to chop and dice the needed ingredients. When they moved to the kitchen, Bridget stood slightly behind Wesley to peer over his shoulder as he explained the importance of using a wooden spoon instead of plastic while working over high heat.

"Carcinogens," he'd said. "Best to avoid whenever possible."

A precaution with which Bridget most heartily agreed. She never wanted to come anywhere near cancer again so long as she lived. Wesley didn't know what had killed her mother, which made it easier to breeze right past his friendly little warning and focus on making the food.

As they continued, he also insisted medium heat would be gentler on the onions and that constant stirring wasn't necessary but preferred.

"Where'd you learn to cook like this?" she asked as she watched him maneuver around the stove with a level of skill she would never attain.

"Around," he answered simply before announcing his next great culinary tip. Maybe she could ask him again later. Right now she was in too much awe to look away from the masterful food coming together right before her very eyes.

She couldn't wait to taste-test it.

Chapter 24

Bridget had assumed a rice-based dish would be easier to prepare than a fancy curry, but she soon found out how many extra steps went into making the *biryani*. They'd even had to use the oven, for crying out loud!

If Wesley weren't there to guide her, she definitely would have messed up some part of it. She'd never been a bad cook, but she'd never embarked on such an ambitious new cuisine before, either. It probably would have helped if she'd eaten Indian food more than a handful of times before attempting to master it in the kitchen.

Wesley, however, seemed to have no issues. It was as if he didn't even need the recipe that Bridget had carefully printed out and brought along with her cooking supplies.

"You need to come today," she said as he pulled out the perfectly browned rice dish and unleashed the wonderful scents of coriander, saffron, and clarified butter into his apartment. "There's no way I can take credit for doing all this on my own, not after last week. You should come and bask in the glory of your culinary prowess."

Wesley let out a full-bellied laugh, his head arched forward in front of his chest. "The glory of my culinary prowess, huh? You make me sound like a Greek god or something."

She grabbed a fork from the counter and dipped it into the dish to steal a bite. "The Greek god of cooking. That's you. Or is it the Indian god?" She lifted the fork in a salute, then shoved the steaming morsel past her lips.

Wesley smirked as he watched her. "That's hot, by the way."

Yup. Of course it was. Bridget should have known. She tried to keep her face straight even as her eyes teared from the heat.

He laughed again when she shot him the thumbs-up sign. "*You* are ridiculous." He pointed to her with the wooden spoon, then turned it back to himself. "And *I* don't need to bask in anything, glory or otherwise."

Bridget was having far too good a time with Wesley for things to end now. What if he turned back into ice man the next time they got together? She liked the warm, smart, laughing Wesley and didn't want him to be replaced with that other guy. Not if she could help it.

"I know they'd love to meet you, and this week is definitely the easiest, since it's at my place," she argued. "Potluck Club won't be here again for another four weeks."

Wesley shifted toward the sink and lifted the tap so that he could begin cleaning up the dirtied pots and utensils.

"No pressure, though," Bridget added as she watched him and tried to figure out why he was so hesitant to accept her invite. After all, he was the one who'd practically begged her to become friends. He was also the one who had suggested they cook together today. "It's an invitation. Not a prison sentence."

Wesley flinched, then slammed the handle down and took a giant step back. "I almost forgot I have something for you. Just a sec while I go get it," he mumbled, disappearing so quickly she didn't even have time to ask for more details.

She stood on her own as Wesley retreated into what she assumed was the bedroom. Strange how the simple thought of enjoying a potluck lunch with her friends sent him running straight out of the room.

Wesley was gone for several minutes, and Bridget had begun to question whether she should follow him in there or give up and head home. Neither seemed like the right response, so she continued to wait.

When he returned, he held an adorable plush toy over his face and wiggled it from side to side. "It's just a small thing, but I saw it and thought of you," Wesley said, lowering the stuffed animal to reveal a gigantic smile on his face.

She squealed in delight as he handed her the gift, then laughed as she noticed that the stuffed dog was wearing a tiny lion hoodie complete with a fluffy mane. "Aww. He looks just like Teddy. Where did you find him?"

Wesley watched her carefully, his smile never faltering. "They have them all over the bookstore. This dog has more outfits than Barbie, I swear. That's Boo, by the way. He's supposed to be the world's cutest dog."

"Boo who?" Bridget asked, laughing at her own joke, then sobering when she realized Wesley's large smile remained unmoving, almost as if it were plastic.

"Nah, it's totally Teddy. And I love it. Thank you so much." She gave him a quick hug, feeling heat tug at her cheeks and her core both. "I hate to run, but I need to be home in case someone comes by early, and either Amy or Nichole almost always does. You sure you don't want to come?"

She wanted him there despite the merciless teasing she knew they'd both endure at the hands of her friends. Wesley had said he didn't want to make friends, but he needed them, needed her. He'd given her a gift, and now she wanted to do the same for him.

The only reason she'd gotten through the obvious walls surrounding him was her bullish determination not to take no for an answer. If Wesley had others in his life, Bridget had never seen them come around, which led her to believe he'd closed out everyone. If only she could figure out why. . . .

His unnatural smile finally faded, and he turned away, mumbling, "I'm not good with new people."

She laughed as she remembered their first dozen exchanges. "Yeah, maybe so. But you're not new to them. They've already heard lots about you from me."

He raised one eyebrow playfully, a bit of the tension swept away once more. "Oh? Like what?"

She wagged her finger at him, then hooked it in a *come hither* gesture. "If you come, I can pretty much guarantee they'll tell you."

"Well, now, I guess that's an offer I can't refuse."

Chapter 25

Wesley helped carry the two freshly prepared dishes back to her apartment. He also carried her largely untouched spices and cooking supplies, leaving her with only the small stuffed animal to transport.

They'd had just enough time to wipe down the counters and set up a serving station when the first of Bridget's friends arrived for their weekly get-together.

Amy's eyes lit immediately upon noticing the handsome newcomer. "Is this him?" she whispered in Bridget's ear while leaning in to give her a hug hello.

"Please don't embarrass me too much," Bridget whispered back, even though she knew it was already too late to hope for such a thing.

Amy spun toward Wesley and threw her arms around him as if greeting a long-lost friend. "It's so good to meet you!" she exclaimed. "I can't wait to hear all about how you know our Bridget."

Bridget rolled her eyes and shrugged helplessly, but Wesley just laughed. Unlike earlier at his apartment, this gesture of happiness appeared completely genuine. "I don't think anyone's ever been so happy to meet me in all my life," he said.

Amy hit him playfully. "Well, I bet that's not true, but tell you what? I'll call my boyfriend over so you're not the only guy at club today. Strength in numbers, right?"

As soon as Amy picked up her phone, Nichole appeared at the door. "Hello again, stranger," she said with a small smile. She didn't offer Wesley a hug, but she did twitch her nose in curiosity and storm straight into the kitchen.

Finding what she'd been looking for, she stared at the two dishes Wesley and Bridget had prepared in open horror. "Oh, B! Please tell me you didn't try making Indian food again. It wasn't even edible last week!"

"Hey," Bridget cried. "I tried my best, but I'm still learning. And for your information, Wesley helped me this time and he's a professional, so you all need to shush."

"You're a chef?" Amy asked, returning her attention to the people in the room with her. "I love that. I used to work in a bakery for extra money during my college days."

"More of a short-order cook," Wesley corrected. "But I do love sharing my . . . What was it, Bridget? Oh, right . . . *the glory of my culinary prowess* with others."

"You fit right in already," Nichole said, patting him on the shoulder and tossing a wink toward Bridget.

"She's right," Amy added. "We definitely don't tease B as much as we probably should."

"Really, I think you guys do just fine on your own," Bridget said with a groan.

That's when Hazel showed up. "Fine with what?" she asked Bridget before noticing Wesley and marching right up to him. "Oh, hello there. Is this the hot guy we saw from your window before?" she asked, facing Wesley but glancing over her shoulder as she addressed Bridget.

And now she officially wanted to run into her bedroom, lock the door, and hide under the covers until this whole thing was over.

Wesley extricated himself from the crowd by the door and took a seat at the dining table. "Bridget and I run together," he explained. "I live on the first floor."

Amy pumped her head, clearly recalling the conversation she and Bridget had had over cookies. "And you have dogs, right?"

He smiled as he studied his hands on the table before him. "Two. A husky named Beau and a malamute named Snow. For Jon Snow."

"Nice," Nichole said, taking a seat across from Wesley at the table. "So what else do we need to know about you?"

"Enough with the questions!" Bridget cried. "You're going to scare him away!" She could already see him retreating into himself, and that was the exact opposite of her purpose in inviting him here.

"We have to put him through the gauntlet to make sure he's strong enough to stick around," Hazel explained.

Wesley's eyes shot up from the table and searched the room until they landed on Hazel. "Gauntlet? What else have you got planned besides questions and friendly conversation?"

"Oh, you'll see soon enough!" Hazel said with an evil laugh.

"Should I be afraid?" Wesley asked Bridget, smiling at least.

"Probably."

"Oh, stop. All the guys have to go through this. It's not like you went easy on Trent or Keith," Amy scolded but laughed anyway. "Besides Trent and his daughter, Olivia, will be here soon, and that will take some of the heat off you. They could both use some yummy food after three days of only eating meals that could be cooked over a campfire. For that matter, so can I." She touched her belly, frowned, and then scurried into the kitchen to start their weekly feast.

"There's an important difference here. Wesley and I are

just friends. Keith and Trent both came into the group as boy-friends."

"And now fiancé and future fiancé," Hazel added with a sharp glance toward Amy.

"You better not say that in front of him!" Amy cried around a mouthful of whatever baked good she'd brought.

"Where'd you go to college, Wesley?" Nichole asked, bringing all eyes back to their guest.

"I started at UAA but wasn't ever able to finish."

"I went to UAA, too," Nichole said with a nod. "What years were you there?"

"Guys, conversation is fine, but interrogation is not."

"Oh, relax, B!"

"You said you like *Game of Thrones*, Wesley?" Amy asked, taking a seat at the table with her neatly arranged plate. "Just the TV show or the books, too?"

Wesley smirked in that way a true fan does whenever asked about an adaptation of something he fell in love with in its original format. "The show was great, but it didn't do the books justice."

"Right answer." Amy made a clicking sound and pointed to Wesley with a giant, relieved smile.

That started a lengthy conversation on who most deserved the iron throne and whether dire wolves would make good pets in the real world. Wesley and Amy were discussing casting choices for the HBO series when her boyfriend, Trent, arrived with Olivia in tow.

"Hi, Trent!" She rushed over to greet him with a tight hug and a chaste kiss. Amy was always more careful about how she showed her affection when Olivia was around; after all, she had been the girl's teacher last year.

"Hi, Liv!" she said, hugging the girl just as tight. "This is Bridget's new friend, Wesley."

Olivia giggled. "I know what that means."

Wesley waved from his spot at the table rather than coming over to shake hands, which Bridget found a bit odd. She also found it odd that Trent kept shooting glances at Wesley when he thought no one was looking.

But Bridget was always looking.

Did these two know each other already?

It sure seemed that way. . . .

Chapter 26

Everyone loaded up their plates with that week's eclectic mix of potluck cuisine, then those who could fit crowded around Bridget's dining table. The others settled in the living room.

Although Bridget had secured a seat at the table, Wesley had not. So while Olivia and Amy regaled the group with their camping adventures of the past week, Bridget slipped away to join the men on the couch.

Trent and Wesley sat as far away from each other as possible, leaving plenty of space for Bridget to plop between the two of them. Neither had eaten much of anything, and they didn't appear to be talking, either. Instead, they stared down at the loaded plates in their laps and wore matching expressions—blank, impassive, yet somehow also pained.

If they knew each other, it seemed both would rather forget it.

It also seemed that breaking the tension in this room would fall to Bridget. As much as she preferred the weeks when one of the other members hosted their weekly get-together, she still didn't want to see her gathering fall to pieces almost as soon as it had started.

Swallowing down a bite of biryani, she balanced her fork

carefully on the rim of the plate, then slung an arm over each of the men's shoulders. "Wesley, I know you're new here, but, Trent, you should definitely know better. No one stays quiet during a Potluck Club meeting, and no one leaves hungry. C'mon, guys. Don't break our perfect streak."

She chortled, but neither man joined in or attempted to explain what had them so upset that one had turned to ice and the other to granite.

"This was a mistake," Wesley said, untangling himself from Bridget and getting to his feet. "I shouldn't have come."

Trent cleared his throat but remained quiet as he watched the other man with a cold, hard stare. Bridget had begged Wesley to join her, but now everything was falling to pieces and she had no idea why.

Where was Amy? Couldn't she help rein them in?

"Wesley, wait," Bridget called as she jumped up and hurried after him, but he was already at the door, pulling it open and striding away.

"Wait!" she cried again, stepping out into the hall and pulling the door shut behind her. "What happened? Why are you going?"

Wesley froze at the head of the stairs but didn't turn to face her. His entire body shook as if a sudden chill had swept through the hallway. Impossible in this stiff summer air. Then again, everything about this afternoon felt as if it couldn't possibly be happening, couldn't possibly be real.

Bridget approached him slowly, hoping not to frighten him away or to make this—*whatever it was*—any worse. "I don't understand," she said softly. "Do you and Trent know each other somehow?"

"I shouldn't have come," he said, repeating the same words he'd spoken before. His body stiffened, and she could already sense him closing off; somehow, it was even worse than it had been in the beginning. This wasn't her Wesley. Not at all.

Bridget reached out and touched his elbow; he didn't make any move to tear it away. A small glimmer of hope?

"You're my friend. I want you here. That's why I invited you—okay, practically *begged* you—to come. If Trent did something to make you—"

"No," Wesley interrupted her. He took a few steps down the stairs before finally turning to face her. His eyes had transitioned to that dark, ominous shade of blue, the one she hadn't seen in a while, now that they'd been getting along so well. This afternoon, his icy demeanor was back, but she could see sorrow surging just beneath the surface, trying desperately to break through while he worked so hard to keep it behind the emotional dam he'd constructed.

Then, as if suddenly changing his mind, he jogged back up the stairs and lifted a hand to Bridget's cheek.

She leaned her face into his palm and closed her eyes. When she opened them again, she saw tears gathering, brimming, but still not falling.

"Just promise me," he whispered, bringing his face near. "Promise me that whatever he says about me, you'll see me for the man you got to know yourself."

"What?" She stared at him as the fat, hot tears forming in her own eyes turned him into a blur. Now she couldn't recognize his face or his words. How could weeks of building their relationship be suddenly undone by a few minutes while he sat beside Trent in her living room?

"Promise me, Bridget," he croaked, his voice desperate, pleading.

"I p-p-promise," she sputtered. "But, Wesley, what is he going to say? I'd rather hear it from you."

He shook his head and took a step back, forgetting the stairs and stumbling down a few before catching himself again.

She moved to help him, but he held up a hand to stop her.

The apartment door opened, and Amy joined Bridget in the hall. "Bridget, come back inside," she urged, her delicate features pinched, making them seem even smaller. She looked so fragile, and yet she'd come to protect Bridget. *From what?*

"But, Wesley . . ." Bridget argued, unsure of what she could say as she searched her friend's expression to see if she understood any of what was going on.

"He's already gone," Amy whispered, grabbing Bridget's wrist and pulling her back to the door.

When Bridget glanced back toward the stairs, she saw nothing, understood nothing. But felt the weight of it all crash down on her all the same.

She felt so many things in that moment. Worry for her new friend, mostly. Confusion as to what possibly could have happened between Trent and Wesley to cause this scene. And questions, so many questions. First, a question as to why her heart was breaking as she felt Wesley's absence envelop her. A terrible physical thing, like a blanket that had once comforted but now strangled.

Why couldn't she breathe?

And what about Wesley? Was he feeling like this, too? Worse?

Would she ever see him again?

And was she ready to hear whatever Trent had to say?

Chapter 27

Back in the apartment, Bridget's guests sat staring fixedly at the door. When she entered, they all sprang to action. Had that short time in the hall really been enough for them to understand what Bridget still didn't?

Hazel rose from her seat and grabbed her purse from the counter, not meeting Bridget's eyes as she went. "C'mon, Olivia, let's go pick up some ice-cream cones for everyone," she murmured.

The little girl cheered and followed Hazel away. At the same time, Nichole moved to the kitchen to begin cleaning up, and Amy moved to the couch to sit beside Trent.

"What's going on?" Bridget asked with wide eyes. She felt her own body shaking, much as Wesley's had when he stood facing away from her on the stairs. Everyone in here was facing away from her, too.

Once Hazel and Olivia had made their exit, someone finally met Bridget's eyes. It was Amy. Her expression was soft and apologetic as she invited Bridget to enter her own living room. "Trent has something he needs to share with you."

What if I don't want to hear it? What if I want things to go back to how they were exactly one hour ago?

Bridget lowered herself to the carpeted floor and crossed her legs. When her dogs didn't immediately pile on top of her, she scanned the apartment in search of them. She needed their love, strength, and quiet reassurance for whatever came next.

Oh, right. They'd been put in the bedroom for the eating portion of today's get-together. It was the only way to guarantee they wouldn't help themselves to her guests' meals. She always did the same when her turn to host came around, but then again, nothing like this had ever happened before.

And most frustrating of all, she still didn't know what *this* was.

"I've got them," Nichole said from the kitchen. Apparently, her full attention hadn't been on the dishes after all. Everyone's eyes lingered on Bridget as they all waited to see if the coming news would break her.

Amy regarded her with a pinched mouth, sudden pallor overtaking her complexion. Meanwhile, Trent's features had hardened, his heavy brow and granite jaw revealing a side of him she'd never seen before now. Normally, he wore a goofy, open smile and doted on Amy and Olivia for all to see. Bridget had always found it difficult to believe he spent his days working as a prison guard.

Until now.

Now she understood.

Baby and Rosco burst into the living room and tackled Bridget with giant, slobbery licks and a cloud of dog fur. Teddy, however, seemed to know something was wrong. He stiffened and let out a low growl, moving a few steps ahead of Bridget in what appeared to be an effort to protect her from Trent.

"It's okay, Teddy. Come here," she said, but the Pomeranian remained rooted to the spot, ready to strike the man he'd considered a friend at every other encounter.

"Go ahead and tell her," Amy urged, wedging each of her slim fingers between Trent's much stronger digits.

"That man," he began, then cleared his throat and started again. "That man is not a good friend for you to have."

"Why?" she challenged, refusing to take him at his word. Trent might mean a lot to Amy, but Bridget didn't know him all that well herself. Could she really trust his word without any evidence?

Of course not. And she wouldn't.

"I shouldn't say," he hedged.

"Either say it or don't, but unless you give me a really good reason, I'm not going to stop seeing Wesley."

Trent turned red but said nothing.

"It's okay," Amy said, giving his hand a squeeze and turning his fingers red, too. "I'll tell her."

"Tell me what?" Bridget demanded. She was so very tired of everyone knowing but her.

Amy took a deep breath and let it out slowly.

Bridget felt the seconds tick away like the countdown on a bomb, one that would cause unforeseen destruction in her world. She had half a mind to charge out of the apartment and seek Wesley for whatever explanation was coming. She wanted to hear whatever it was directly from her friend himself, not from her other friend's boyfriend.

But then Amy spoke. "B, sweetie. Trent already knows Wesley."

"Yeah, I gathered that much. How do they know each other?"

"From work," Amy said, swallowing another giant gulp of air that somehow made her face appear even more ruddy.

"But how?" Bridget asked, feeling more confused than ever. "Wesley's a cook, and Trent's a . . ." *Trent was a prison guard.*

Amy nodded, shooting Bridget a meaningful look, willing her to understand, to stop asking questions and just accept what they were trying to tell her.

Trent remained silent, probably already having said way more than he was allowed.

"Oh," Bridget whispered. *Trent was a prison guard, and Wesley had been a prisoner.*

"He never told me that," she insisted, feeling so deceived in that moment. And he hadn't, but it explained so much. Why he was hesitant to make new friends, what he was running away from each night, even the way he kept his apartment—small, tidy, sparse. It also explained why he often trailed off and disappeared into himself in conversations.

Had he wanted to tell her but hadn't yet found the right time? Or had he deliberately hidden this huge, important thing about himself?

Nichole drifted into the room and sat beside Bridget on the floor. "Are you okay?" she asked, touching her friend's knee.

"Yeah. I mean, why wouldn't I be? He was probably just in for drugs or marijuana, right? That's not such a big deal. I bet—"

"No," Trent interrupted, his expression finally softening. "It wasn't drugs. And it is a big deal."

Amy stroked Trent's arm, because apparently he needed comfort just as much as Bridget now. "Of course Trent and the others do everything they can to help rehabilitate their prisoners, but the truth is that many of them return to their old ways."

"Wesley isn't like that," Bridget argued, but her quavering voice betrayed her. "You don't know him like I do. He's a good guy, and he would never—"

"He was in for a violent crime, Bridget," Trent said, slicing through her argument with ease. "Someone almost died. If she had, his sentence would have been much, much longer."

"*She?* But I don't understand." Horror swept through her. Could Wesley have really hurt someone so severely? Could he have hurt someone at all? It didn't fit, but she could also see the truth reflected in Trent's eyes, the shocking reveal mirrored in Wesley's posture during their exchange in the hall.

He had done it. And he'd lied. Hidden.

Would he have hurt her one day, too? Could he have?

Trent sank back on the couch, depleted. "The details don't matter. I've already said too much, but please just trust me on this one. You're like a sister to Amy, which means you're family to me. I need you to be safe."

Bridget swallowed hard and then nodded. "Okay."

Because what else could she say? What else could she do?

Chapter 28

After Olivia and Hazel returned with strawberry sundaes for everyone, Bridget made a big show of eating and enjoying hers for the little girl's sake. Olivia had suffered enough the past couple years, both losing her mother and then moving far from her home to resettle in Anchorage. She didn't need to take on the weight of Bridget's problems on top of everything else.

Bridget didn't even feel equipped to deal with this latest shock to her life. Her insides burned hot with rage, disappointment, betrayal despite the cool comfort her favorite guilty pleasure normally offered.

Her friends downed their sundaes so quickly, it was a wonder they didn't all end up with incurable cases of brain freeze. Once finished, they raced to the door in what was practically a stampede, which suited Bridget just fine. She needed some time alone to unravel what she'd just learned.

Amy, however, lingered.

"I'm staying with you tonight," she announced without preamble. "Do you have some PJs I could borrow?"

"Come with me," Bridget said, hardly even upset anymore as she guided her friend to her bedroom and fished out a pair of old sweats. While Amy was a good deal taller than Bridget, she was also thinner, so hopefully the clothes would fit.

Amy went to change in the bathroom while Bridget searched her closet for a spare set of bedding. She found a comforter and pillow balled up on the top shelf, and she pulled them down. The cardboard box beside them was dislodged and fell to the floor.

Her mother's box.

"Oh, shoot. Let me help you with that." Amy raced over and lifted the box before Bridget could stop her. "Hmm. This is way lighter than I thought it would be. What's in here?"

Bridget hopped to her feet and yanked her mother's box away from Amy before she could shake it up and down again. Nothing inside was breakable, and yet . . .

"Sorry," Amy said, her cheeks red.

"It's fine. Just best not to bounce it." She left Amy in her room while she searched the apartment for a better place to stash the box. On the floor of the closet, her dogs would be able to get to it. And if she put it back at the top of her closet, Amy might go looking for it—or it could fall down again. The last thing she needed was to be forced to go through the contents because of an unintended spill.

Finally, Bridget made a place for the box under the bathroom sink by pushing the jumble of lotions, soaps, and hair supplies to the very back of the cabinet. She even grabbed a garbage bag from the kitchen and carefully draped it over the box to ensure that no damage would come to it.

Back in her room, Amy sat on the bed waiting with tears in her eyes. "I'm sorry, B!"

Bridget was just about to apologize for overreacting, but then Amy wailed again.

"I shouldn't have teased you so much or pushed you toward Wesley. It's just that day when you came to visit, I could tell how much you liked him, even though you weren't saying it. I thought you were like me and Trent, but I was wrong. So very wrong."

"It's not your fault," she said, finding it odd that she needed to comfort her friend when she was the one who had been wronged. "If it weren't for you and Trent, I still wouldn't know who he really is."

Amy sniffed and nodded. "So you forgive me?"

"I was never mad to begin with. At least not at you." Truth be told, Bridget still didn't know exactly how she felt since learning the truth about Wesley's past. She wished she could ask him about it directly, but she'd also made a promise to Trent that she'd stay away.

What confused her most of all, though, was why Wesley had changed his mind about her. He'd kept her at a distance for weeks until suddenly it seemed he would do anything it took to close the gap. She'd enjoyed their time together— even crushed on him a little—but why would he allow her to get close if he knew what would eventually happen?

Unless he'd planned to keep his criminal past a secret from her forever.

As it was, she still didn't know what he'd done. She'd also never seen anything in him that suggested violent tendencies. When he was upset, he backed away, forcing his emotions inside rather than flying forward in rage.

Which begged the question: Could Trent be mistaken?

No, that wasn't possible, either. Wesley had recognized him, too. He'd run away and asked not to be judged because of whatever Trent decided to share with her.

But hadn't Wesley already judged her and deemed her unworthy of hearing his secret? Or if not unworthy, at least incapable of understanding?

She hadn't asked for any of this. In fact, she'd tried hard to avoid it. She'd been perfectly content as Wesley's running partner. He was the one who had pushed for more.

This was all his fault. He'd forced his way into her confidence but hadn't let her into his. He'd done whatever it was that landed him in prison, and he'd run away from her rather than confront the truth.

His fault, yes. Now she *was* angry.

And even as she tried to convince herself that she'd be better off without him, she couldn't help but feel that niggling sense of doubt poking at her heart. She'd expected so much more from Wesley, so much more from herself.

It was like she hadn't learned anything at all.

Chapter 29

A night of chick flicks and junk food helped to keep Bridget's anger at bay. As soon as she returned to normal life the next day, however, that same immense feeling of betrayal returned. She could hardly focus on making friendly small talk with pet owners as her job required. Dr. Kate shot her meaningful glances throughout the day, but luckily Bridget managed to escape the clinic without having to either confide in or lie to her boss.

She wanted to believe that she could push Wesley from her mind and move forward as if he'd never entered her life at all. But she also knew herself better than that. Memories piled up in her heart like the calories from mint chocolate chip ice cream on her hips.

By the time six o'clock rolled around, she'd made up her mind.

Closure, that's what she needed.

After all, Wesley owed her at least that much.

She left her dogs at home and made her way out to the courtyard. As expected, Wesley appeared a moment later, with Beau and Snow trailing him on their leashes. He wore a bulky pair of headphones and kept his eyes straight ahead, not once flicking them toward Bridget.

"Hey!" She charged after him, refusing to let him escape without acknowledging her. He owed her so much, and yet he couldn't muster up basic good manners? Regardless of their history, she was still a human being and she deserved his respect, if nothing else.

"Hey!" she called again, louder this time.

Wesley stepped to the side and continued down the path. He still wouldn't raise his eyes to meet hers.

No, you don't get to erase me from my own life!

Every bit of anger, confusion, and hurt she'd stockpiled since Trent's big reveal bubbled to the surface at once, and Bridget shoved Wesley hard from behind.

He stumbled forward, then spun toward her, yanking his headphones down so they sat on his neck like a collar. "What do you want, Bridget?" Despite the jerkiness of his movements, his voice came out cold, fluid.

Bridget laughed sarcastically. "What do you mean what do I want? I'd think it would be very obvious."

He sighed and shook his head, pulled his headphones back on.

She ripped them away and hurled them to the ground. "How about an explanation, or at least an apology?"

Snow, who had always been friendly with Bridget, lowered his head and emitted a low, defensive growl.

Wesley jerked the leash to silence him. "I'm not going to apologize for my past. What's the point? There's no changing it. And there's obviously no changing your mind about it, either."

"But you're not even trying," she exploded, crossing her arms over herself, partially in defense and partially to avoid shoving him again. "You have no idea how I feel or what I think about all this."

He glowered at her. "Don't I? Because this thing we're doing here"—he motioned between the two of them rapidly—"that makes it pretty clear."

"You're the one who hid things from me. You're the one who lied."

"I never lied." He said each word slowly and then clenched his jaw and narrowed his eyes at her, showing her the first glimpse of the criminal she still couldn't believe he'd been.

She stooped down and picked up his headphones, but kept them tight in her fist. "You never told me the truth, either. You let Trent do it for you. What are you so afraid of, huh?"

"I don't have time for this," he hissed, and turned away from her once again.

Bridget grabbed at his wrist and missed. "No wonder you didn't want to be friends. You're not capable of it. Are you?" she shouted as his pace quickened, as he and the arctic dogs raced away from her. "Hey, you forgot your headphones!"

Even that wasn't enough to keep him, not enough to make him fight for their friendship. Had he ever really cared about her at all? It didn't feel that way now.

Where was the man who'd patiently taught her how to make Indian food the day before? Where was the running partner who altered his pace to match hers but never once made her feel bad about needing to go slow? What about the neighbor who had brought her soup when her sorrows had prevented her from joining him in the courtyard?

Bridget's tears came hot and fast. None of those versions of him had been real. This was the real Wesley, the one before her now, the one running away rather than trusting her with the truth. She didn't matter to him, probably never had.

"You're a bad person, Wesley Wright," she screamed, just as he and his dogs reached the corner. "The worst kind of person, and it's not because of your past, but because of this, what you're doing right now."

She tossed his headphones on the bench seat and dragged herself back to the apartment.

She hated Wesley for doing this to her.

She hated herself for letting someone else in when she knew better.

That was her life now, keeping new people out and hoping the ones she'd already let in wouldn't suddenly fall sick or change into unrecognizable monsters.

Teddy licked at her tears. His little pink tongue tickled as he frantically lapped the saltwater tracks from her cheeks.

People would always let her down, because that's what people did. Even her father, brothers, friends would find ways to hurt her. She knew that, and she also knew that she would forgive them when it happened.

Wesley, though, he didn't want her forgiveness. He didn't want any part of her at all. So then why did her heart yearn for him even now?

Chapter 30

A loud, consistent banging from the other side of Bridget's door made the keys on the hook beside it jangle. She checked the time on her microwave clock. *Eight P.M.*

It had been two hours since she'd confronted Wesley in the courtyard. Two hours since she'd decided to lose herself in a Netflix binge, to immerse herself in the characters' problems in the hopes of forgetting hers. And now her problems had turned up at her front door. She knew it couldn't be Wesley, and she really didn't feel like talking to anyone else.

"What do you want?" she shouted at whomever was on the other side of that door.

The visitor continued to pound on the wood, but she hardly heard it over the ruckus of her dogs' excited barking. If it really was Wesley waiting on the other side, would the three of them jump to her defense? They didn't even know what had happened or why there would be no more running. Poor things.

She groaned and pulled herself off the couch.

Hazel stood with her fist raised, ready to knock again. When she saw Bridget, she lowered her hand and flexed it.

"About time," she grumbled. "I swear my knuckles are about to rip open from all that knocking."

"What are you doing here?"

"You weren't answering your phone, so here I am." Hazel squeezed past Bridget into the apartment and made her way straight to the kitchen.

"It must have been on silent," Bridget said, clicking the door shut behind her friend and making sure to activate both locks before heading over to join Hazel in the kitchen.

"I brought more ice cream, just in case you were out, and I see that was the right call." Hazel placed a fresh container of mint chocolate chip—this time Häagen-Dazs—in Bridget's hands with a smile. These past couple days, Bridget had practically eaten her body weight in her favorite minty green ice cream, and apparently that would continue, thanks to Hazel.

"What are we watching?" Hazel said, plopping down onto the couch and unpausing Bridget's show.

"Um, don't you have a wedding to be planning?" Bridget tried. She just wanted to be alone. Why couldn't her friends respect that?

Hazel shrugged. "I do, but I'm taking a night off to make sure you're okay."

"No need. As you can see, I'm just fine."

Her friend laughed sarcastically. "Now I know you couldn't possibly believe that. Come sit, eat some ice cream, and tell me what's on your mind. By the way, today's my shift, but tomorrow, you're stuck with Nichole."

Bridget groaned. She didn't want to appear unappreciative, but she also didn't feel the need to talk about her feelings when there was nothing she could do about them until Wesley finally deigned to talk to her. "Why do you guys need to take shifts? Why do you even need to be here at all?"

"Because you're our best friend and you've been through

a lot and we worry, so come take a load off and tell big sis Hazel how we can make it better."

Bridget rolled her eyes but finally settled back onto the couch.

Hazel pulled her knees up to her chest and turned toward Bridget, her eyes wide. "So, tell me, how's work?" Apparently, they were going to dance around the reason Hazel had come, the reason Amy had stayed last night and Nichole would be here tomorrow.

"Work is fine. Busy. The usual."

"And how's the shelter?"

"Fine. Busier than usual." Uh-oh. She should not have said that. Hazel was far too good at picking up details to let that one go by.

Sure enough, her friend leaned forward, her eyes wide. "Oh, why?"

"I may have gotten volunteered to lead another big event, and it's in less than three weeks now."

Hazel gasped and leaned closer. "What? Why didn't you tell us?"

"I didn't want you to feel obligated to help." Bridget looked away, heat rushing to her cheeks as she remembered that she had more than one big problem weighing on her right now.

"Girl, you know we're happy to help! How far into it are you?"

Bridget chewed her lip as she considered whether it would do any good to lie about the situation. It wouldn't. "Well, I have an idea, but that's about it."

Hazel pretended to faint dead against the couch. "Oh my, then it's a good thing I'm here. Should I call the others over, too?"

"No, no, no. I've got this." That at least wasn't a lie, because one way or another, Bridget would handle the situation.

Hazel liked to be the one who handled things, though, especially where her friends were concerned. "Like heck you do! We're obviously all pitching in to help, so tell me what I can do."

"Tonight, can you just be my friend?" Bridget asked glumly.

"Oh, my sweet B." Hazel crawled toward her and gave her a warm hug. "I always am, no matter what. You must feel so awful after everything that happened with Wesley, but just know that you can always trust me and the girls. Keith and Trent, too."

"I know that," Bridget mumbled into her friend's hair. "It's still hard. It's hard on the dogs, too. They were so disappointed when we didn't go running tonight."

"Can't you still go running without him?"

She shook her head gently. "I could, but it would be weird. It would be like being with him without, you know, being with him."

"Hey, wait a sec." Hazel pulled back, her eyes glowing with whatever new idea had sparked in her brain. "When you chose this apartment, you told us there was a weekly walking club for the residents and their dogs. Why don't you do that instead? It might be nice to meet other neighbors."

"That's a good idea, except the club closed down. The woman who ran it bought a house and moved away. And no one wanted to step up to be the new leader." Bridget knew, because she'd asked the landlord right after she signed her lease. It had been a huge selling point for her when choosing this apartment, and yet the group didn't even exist any longer.

Hazel didn't seem bothered by this problem. She probably already had a solution for it. She smiled wide and asked, "How about you? This kind of thing is right in your wheelhouse."

Of course.

"Remember how I have less than three measly weeks to plan a huge fundraiser for the shelter?" Bridget had let herself forget as she struggled to make sense of the Wesley situation, and that just wasn't fair to the animals. She needed to stop worrying about her own messed-up life and focus on the cats and dogs who needed her attention so much more.

Hazel's smile faltered and her eyes narrowed as she went into battle mode. "Oh, yeah. You need to ask for more time."

"I can't do—"

"You want it to be successful, right? No harm in asking for more time. And while you do that, I'm calling in reinforcements."

Chapter 31

Nichole and Amy turned up at Bridget's apartment about half an hour later. They both brought ice cream, too.

"We got your SOS. What's up?" Nichole asked after she'd stormed inside and swept through the apartment to make sure no one was severely injured.

Hazel motioned toward Bridget with a dramatic flourish. "Bridget has to put on another big event for the shelter and has about two and a half weeks to plan it from start to finish."

"B! Are you serious? Didn't you learn anything from the last time?" Nichole demanded, already diving into her oversized bag to pull out her favorite notebook and get to work making one of her infamous lists.

Hazel placed a hand on Bridget's shoulder in a show of support. "She wasn't the one to volunteer this time. Someone else did that for her."

Amy actually looked hurt by this revelation. "How long have you known, and why didn't you come to us sooner?"

Bridget felt as if she'd been sent to the principal's office because another student had been caught cheating from her test. Yes, this was bad, but it also wasn't her fault. Still, she couldn't quite meet Amy's eyes, either. "A couple days ago, and I didn't want to bother you guys. I thought—"

"You thought wrong," Nichole said with a scowl. "Tell us how we can help." She flipped to a fresh page of her notebook and held her pen at the ready.

Hazel seamlessly took command of the situation. "She wants to do a charity race, like with sponsors and donations per mile."

"What about the adoptions?" Amy wanted to know.

Everyone looked to Bridget.

Her voice shook before growing stronger. "I thought we could have the race start and end outside the shelter and even bring out some of the friendlier dogs to interact with those waiting for loved ones to run."

"Sounds good so far. Let's make a list of everything we need to make this happen." Hazel pulled out her phone and opened the notes app, but Nichole pushed her hand down.

"I've got my trusty notebook right here."

Amy giggled. "You sound like the *Blue's Clues* guy."

Nichole stuck out her tongue playfully. "And you sound like you've been fully assimilated into mom culture. Isn't Olivia too old for that show, though?"

"I watched it when I was little," she said, shaking her head. "And now they're doing a reboot."

"Yeah, so, anyway . . ." Hazel paused to make sure everyone was paying attention to the task at hand before continuing. "We'll need event T-shirts, signage, a ribbon for the finish line . . . What else?"

"Sponsors," Nichole added, scrawling away furiously on her pad. "And maybe one of those donation thermometers to show how close we are to hitting our goal?"

Hazel nodded her approval. "Perfect. What's our goal?"

Everyone turned back to Bridget again.

She shrugged. "I have no idea. Last time my goal was to get all the pets adopted. This time . . . Well, how much money should we even expect?"

"Didn't the person who volunteered you for this give you any guidance?" Nichole asked, both eyebrows raised.

"I received exactly zero guidance. She basically ambushed me during my shift and told me to put together another big event like we did for Valentine's Day and that she wanted it to happen the first weekend of August."

Nichole tapped her pen on the edge of her notebook, appearing frustrated. "Who is this person? Is she your boss?"

"No, but she is a staffer."

"I've been out of the corporate world for a while," Hazel said thoughtfully. "But in cases like this one, I think it's completely warranted to go over her and speak with her boss about all this."

"Yes, totally," Amy and Nichole agreed, bobbing their heads in unison.

Hazel took Bridget's phone and began scrolling through the contacts. "Do you have the big boss's number? Can you call now?"

Bridget hesitated. "It's almost nine. I don't think—"

"Do you have the number or not?" her friend demanded.

"Yes, I have it, but for emergencies only. He gave it to me when I was working on the last big event."

"I'd say this qualifies as an emergency," Amy pointed out quietly.

"You need to call him now," Nichole said less gently.

Bridget glanced from one friend to the next. "Shouldn't I try Peg first? She's usually the one—"

"Skip the middle management and go straight to the top," Hazel said.

"*Fine,*" Bridget acquiesced with a sigh.

"Put it on speaker," Hazel said right before the head of the board picked up.

"Hello?" David answered on the other end of the call.

Bridget's heart flooded with fear. Would he be upset with her for calling so late? Or for dropping the ball on kicking off the planning?

She took a deep, steadying breath and dove right in. "Hi, David. This is Bridget. I'm so sorry to bother you, but I have a bit of a problem."

"That's okay. I'm up for another few hours at least. What's going on?"

"Well, this event for August, I'm just really struggling to get everything done in time, and—"

"What event? *May's* event?"

"*May's*? Well, she was the one who asked me to put something together and gave me the tight deadline, but . . ." As much as she disliked the older woman, she wouldn't willingly throw her under the bus.

"For the first weekend of August, right? May told me everything was already handled and good to go."

Nichole couldn't stop a sarcastic laugh from escaping. "Hardly."

"Give me the phone," Hazel said before yanking it from Bridget's hands.

"Hello, David. My name is Hazel, and I'm friends with Bridget. It seems this May person has been intentionally misleading both of you, at least as far as this event is concerned." She went on to explain everything that had happened just as Bridget had confided in her earlier that night.

"Wow, I expected better from May," David said, his voice more sad than angry. "Especially after she did such a good job with the cat portion of our Valentine's event."

"But Bridget did that!" the usually mild-mannered Amy shouted.

David chuckled. "I should have known, especially given how weak May's original attempts at putting something together were. . . . Bridget, are you still there?"

Hazel handed the phone back. "Yes, David. I'm here."

"Do me a favor and report to me directly for the August event. Okay?"

"Sure, but is there any way we could have a bit more time? I just found out about this a couple days ago, and I don't even know what our goals are. So not only do I need to plan the event, I also need to figure out how much we're looking to raise and—"

"How's the third weekend instead?" David suggested. "I'll email you some thoughts I have regarding the benchmarks and budget. Think that extra time and guidance will be enough to see you through?"

For the first time in days, Bridget finally felt like she could breathe again. "That's perfect," she said with a smile before hanging up the phone.

Chapter 32

Bridget's friends stayed well past midnight to help her get a head start on the upcoming charity run. She found their company soothing and familiar, but not quite healing.

She still needed to work through all that had happened with Wesley and to determine how much of the whole thing had been her fault rather than his. Her friends couldn't help with this, and she didn't want to involve them in her pain. Although the basis of their relationship had originally been a shared grief, the hurt Wesley had caused belonged to Bridget—and Bridget only.

Would she ever find a way to move past it?

Part of her was desperate to feel like herself again, but another part recognized she hadn't been *herself* in a very long time. Even before losing her mother, something insurmountable had changed inside of her. Maybe that was a part of growing up that everyone had to go through, or maybe she'd been trying to force herself into a life that no longer fit and had only just begun to realize it now.

When a gentle knock sounded on her door at half past six the following evening, she expected to find Nichole, who according to Hazel had been scheduled to keep Bridget company for the night. Instead, she found her dad and Caleb standing side by side; matching grins lit their tanned faces.

They turned to each other, nodded once, then grabbed Bridget and dragged her into the hall.

"Hey," she protested with a nervous laugh. "Why are you kidnapping me from my apartment?"

"Well, don't you catch on fast, Bridgey?" her brother said, pulling her toward the stairs while their father followed. Thank goodness she hadn't changed into her pajamas immediately following work as she'd originally planned.

Her father brought up the rear as Caleb dragged her down the stairs with surprising strength and an unrelenting grip. "Your friend Nichole came to see us, said you needed some extra support, so here we are."

"Yes, here we are, but where are we going?"

"B—"

"Don't tell her, Dad!" Caleb yelled. "It's supposed to be a surprise."

"Are we going bowling?" she asked with another laugh.

Caleb turned to scowl at their father over her shoulder. "You've just gotta give everything away. Don't you?"

"How was your writing conference, Caleb?" Bridget asked as she squeezed into the back seat of her father's old sedan. Caleb always got to ride shotgun because of his much longer legs, and apparently today wouldn't be any different.

"Inspiring," he said, then sighed happily, the same way he'd always done when talking about his latest artistic pursuit. None of those had stuck, and she doubted this one would, either—whether or not he'd been to a professional conference this time around.

"All righty, then." She stayed quiet while her father pulled out of his parking space and navigated onto the main road. "Dad, you said Nichole stopped by. What did she say?"

Caleb twisted in his seat and met Bridget's eyes with a smirk. "She told us everything, Bridgey. Every last secret."

"Oh, hush up, you," her father scolded. "She told us you were having a hard time lately. She didn't give us a ton of details but did mention you were under some pressure at the shelter to pull off a big event with very little lead time."

Bridget let out a breath she hadn't realized she'd been holding, thankful Nichole hadn't mentioned Wesley to her family. She didn't know why she wanted to keep the details of her failed friendship from them, only that it didn't feel right. Nothing felt right when it came to Wesley, not anymore.

"Bridget, did you hear me?" her father asked, turning slightly in his seat and jerking the car toward the shoulder of the road.

"Sorry. What?" She shook her head and forced herself to focus on the conversation rather than continuing to follow the erratic path of her private thoughts.

"I was just kidding about the secrets," Caleb said as he rolled down the windows. "Maybe some fresh air will wake you back up."

Warm air gusted through the car, filling all of Bridget's senses. She'd always loved tasting the sweet summer sky, feeling it on her cheeks.

Her brother waited about a minute and then rolled the windows up again. "Go ahead, Dad," he urged.

Her father cleared his throat. "Oh, I was just wondering if there was anything we could do to help with your fundraising project for the shelter." His voice lilted hopefully. "I don't have much to keep me occupied in the evenings, and if Caleb devoted half the hours to this that he does those silly video games of his, we'll have the whole thing ready in no time."

Bridget laughed hard while her brother rushed to defend his favorite hobby. "That would be nice," she said, once she could talk again. "Thank you, Dad. And Caleb."

"Hey, I didn't agree to anything," her brother corrected. "But I'll help you, if you help me."

She groaned, all too familiar with her brother's sneaky habit of bargaining his way through life. "What do you need?"

"I need feedback on my manuscript. Dad always says it's great and offers no helpful feedback whatsoever."

"Well, it is great!" their father argued. "I'm proud of you."

Caleb rolled his eyes at Bridget in the rearview mirror. "Anyway, I know you won't hesitate to tear me a new one, which is why you're the perfect beta reader."

Their dad took one hand off the steering wheel and flicked Caleb on the cheek. The car swerved.

"Ouch!" Caleb cried, raising a hand to hold his face. "What was that for?"

"We're here because Bridget is already overwhelmed by everything on her plate. You are not going to add something new before we even have a chance to help her!"

A giant smile lit her face, warming her from the outside in. She didn't have to search her thoughts this time. The answer came to her like a flashing neon sign: N-I-C-H-O-L-E.

"Don't worry about it, Dad," she answered with an even wider grin. "I am too busy to help, but I kind of have the perfect person in mind for you, Caleb."

Chapter 33

Bridget stared down at the scuffed red and cream shoes on her feet, wondering if maybe she should incorporate a similar pair into her everyday wardrobe once she could better afford new attire. The dull lighting somehow made the already vivid shoes seem even brighter when compared to her simple jeans and T-shirt ensemble.

Caleb clapped a hand on her back as they made their way toward the assigned lane. "You know you can always come to me with anything. Don't you?"

"Thanks." She picked up a swirly pink ball and stuck her fingers inside. Even though it was one of the smallest on the rack, it still felt way too heavy.

Caleb made an impressive show of reaching straight for the biggest ball there. It dwarfed Bridget's by comparison; they didn't even look like they belonged to the same sport. "Hey, don't write me off like that. I know I'm your screwup big brother, but I love you and I'm here for you. Okay?"

"Okay." She shot him a smile. Caleb hadn't often played the role of protector; their other brother, Devon, had always done that for both of them. She liked knowing she could count on Caleb now, though, especially considering he'd so rarely been able to count on himself.

He met her smile, his eyes crinkling at the edges. "Okay, now let's go catch up with Dad before he tries to start the game without us."

They bowled two games, and Bridget lost spectacularly each time. When they'd finished, her arms ached from the repetitive motion of hurling her small but heavy ball down the lane. Apparently all that running with no strength component to her regular exercise routine had been a mistake. Her lower body had become strong and taut, but her arms were hardly any better than noodles cooked al dente.

"Shall we do another?" their father asked while cracking the knuckles on each hand. "I think I can beat you this time, Caleb."

Caleb chuckled and shook his head. "You haven't even beaten me a single time. Not tonight. Not ever."

"That's because you always call it quits right as my luck begins to turn around." He grinned at his son, then tossed a wink Bridget's way.

"And that's your problem right there." Caleb stood and clapped his father on the back while shaking his head. "Bowling is a game of skill, not luck. Right, Bridgey?"

"Why are you looking at me? I'm even worse than he is." She hooked a thumb at her father and burst out laughing at the goofy face he made in response.

Caleb stretched both arms overhead as if this whole thing bored him. "Tell you what, old man. Let's put that theory of yours to the test. One more game, one more chance for you to show me what you're made of."

"I'm sitting this one out," Bridget said with a yawn. "But I'm here as your cheerleader, Dad!"

As she watched her dad and brother throw themselves headlong into their new match, she couldn't help but smile to herself. Yes, she'd lost a friend when Wesley had ended up being someone different than he'd led her to believe, but she already had a huge support network in her life. From the members of the Sunday Potluck Club, who showed up week after week and whenever she had a crisis that required their help, to her dad and brothers, whom she didn't see as often but had loved all her life.

Yes, she'd lost a major lifeline when they'd buried her mom at the beginning of the year, but that loss had also brought her, Caleb, and their dad closer, given them a fresh chance to get to know each other.

It wasn't always easy, but it was definitely worth it.

By the time the men finished their game, both looked as tired as she felt. Caleb, of course, had won his third of the night.

"But I was closer this time," their father insisted even though he'd only closed the wide gap between their scores by two pins.

"You're getting a little bit better each time. Three years from now, you'll have me whooped."

Their dad reached up and ruffled his son's hair. Although Caleb stood at least six inches taller, he looked like a little boy in that moment.

Bridget's heart swelled with love for them both. She'd been such a mama's girl growing up, spending every spare moment she could at her mother's side. Would she hurt less now if she'd made more time for the men in her life back then, if she hadn't allowed herself to become so attached to— so dependent on—her mom?

Perhaps, but she wouldn't give up a single memory of her mother if she had to do it all over again.

Although she hadn't always been the best, most attentive daughter and sister to them, Caleb and her father loved her, and they were here for her now and that meant everything.

"I guess this concludes this evening's kidnapping," Caleb quipped as they piled back into their father's car.

"Actually, how about we grab some ice cream first?" she suggested with a coy smile.

"Now, there's an idea worth celebrating." Their father turned around in his seat and gave Bridget an enthusiastic thumbs-up. "I say we celebrate with some extra-large mint chocolate chip cones."

Bridget reached forward and gave him a high five. Suddenly she felt as if she'd fallen fifteen years back in time. She was just a little girl and her entire world revolved around her parents, brothers, and whatever collectible had currently captivated the girls in her elementary school. There was no cancer, no Wesley, no Dr. Kate.

Just love.

And ice cream.

Even though she couldn't go back in time, she could always go back to that feeling by spending time with the family who remained. No matter how different they had become over the years, Dad and Caleb's past meshed with hers perfectly.

She was not alone. She never had been.

Chapter 34

Over the next few weeks, Bridget settled into a new routine, one that no longer involved Wesley. Even now, it was crazy to her that she'd let him take up such a large part of her days when they hadn't even known each other that well or that long before everything fell apart.

Her schedule these days—while still hectic—was much healthier. *No more surprises* had become her new mantra. She'd proceed in a straight line toward her goals, no detours for random new hobbies and definitely no turnoffs into romance.

Instead, she now joined her father and brother every Friday night for bowling and had even picked up some small free weights to use while watching her shows. Hazel, Amy, and Nichole all came over regularly to help with the fundraiser and just generally to see how things were going. Even Nichole said that Bridget had made tremendous progress—although on what Bridget wasn't exactly certain.

She was no longer running each night but still longingly eyed the courtyard whenever six o'clock rolled around. She no longer saw Wesley and his dogs pass through on their runs and wondered if he'd given up the hobby, too.

A part of her wished things had gone differently between

them, that he'd at least offered some kind of explanation before disappearing from her life altogether. Another much bigger part felt perfectly content with the way things had turned out. That made it easier to hate him in the aftermath.

When nearly a week had passed without any sight of Wesley or his dogs, Bridget chanced taking a jog with Teddy. She'd liked the feeling of mastering her body, getting all the pieces to work together to move her quickly down the path—legs and heart pumping, lungs filling with air and then letting it go, letting everything go.

And even though life was better—easier—now, she still missed that sense of calming control that came with putting her full attention on something so simple, so primal for a half hour each day.

She and Teddy ran the more scenic route down the forest trails and beneath the vibrant green canopy. Rather than luxuriating in the beauty this time, Bridget felt as if the thick plant life were closing in on them, suffocating them. It probably didn't help that after two weeks without a single cardio session, she'd jumped straight back onto the more difficult route.

The worst part, though, was the fact that Wesley had somehow stayed with her through all of it. She tried to focus on her heart rate, to take in the scenery, to count her footfalls—anything to keep her mind off her missing partner.

But it did no good.

As much as she'd once enjoyed it, running had become inexorably tied to him. This was the thing that had first brought them together, the way they'd spent most of their time in each other's company.

Did that mean that she hadn't ever loved the running itself but rather the time spent at his side?

Ridiculous.

She craved the endorphin rush, the glowing feeling of accomplishment that followed. Not the man who had misled her from the very moment they'd first said hello.

Yes, later she'd been seduced by the cooking and home visits, the adorable plush version of Teddy, which she'd shoved beside her mother's box under the bathroom sink with the other keepsakes she couldn't bear to look at but also couldn't bring herself to throw away.

They'd begun to build something bigger, but only just.

And now she had more important things to think about. Soon her college courses would start back up, but even before that, she had the charity race in a week and Hazel and Keith's wedding a week after that. Unable to choose between her three dearest friends, Hazel had asked Bridget, Amy, and Nichole all to serve as joint maids of honor—and Bridget had the hideous burnt sienna dress to prove it.

Still, she was happy for her friend, even while feeling a bit of jealousy as well. Bridget hadn't wanted a relationship until one had found her all on its own. Maybe she could open her heart to a man once her life settled down again after the wedding and the fundraiser and the start of school.

Maybe she was meant to live out the rest of her days with only friends, family, and a couple dozen rescue pets to fill her days and her heart. Bridget pictured herself with a husband and three squalling children, stepping into the role her mother had lived so effortlessly. She pictured Dr. Kate, married to her career and happy that way. Would Bridget wind up like one of them? What other options were there, really?

Life didn't have to be crazy. It could be simple, honest . . . lonely.

She tightened her grip on Teddy's leash and pushed her feet harder against the pavement, springing herself forward faster. By the time they returned the courtyard, tears had drenched her cheeks. She hadn't even realized when they'd begun to fall, and she didn't know what exactly had caused them.

Were they restorative or the result of finally giving up?

She didn't know that, either.

She knew only that she needed to keep pressing forward one day at a time, and she would.

Chapter 35

The big charity race arrived on a muggy Saturday morning that August. Without those extra two weeks of harried planning, the event would have ended up rather underwhelming. But thanks to the extra time and lots of help from her friends and family, Bridget had managed to pull off something truly spectacular.

It was early yet, but already the crowd outside the shelter surged with excitement as runners of all ages checked in and did a final round of pre-race stretches. If even a quarter of them adopted a pet afterward, all of the animals inside would have new homes by the end of the day. Bridget knew not to get her hopes up when it came to making a clean sweep. The extra money that had begun to come in from the fundraiser and the adoptions that were sure to follow already marked the charity race as a huge success.

Hazel had taken the lead on gathering the business sponsors and designing an enormous banner to mark the start and finish line for the racers. Amy took care of the refreshments while Nichole mapped out the racetrack and placed markers strategically to keep everyone on the path.

Her father and Caleb recruited runners and walkers by

hanging up flyers anywhere and everywhere they could get permission and by running a social media campaign to spread awareness. Yes, her father had adorably opened his Facebook account to help spread the word to his twenty-three friends there and to post news of the race in local interest groups.

This left Bridget to oversee all the finer details, including how they would get guests in to visit the animals and possibly add a new member to the family while they were at it.

"Big morning." David, the head of the board, power walked over to Bridget in teeny-tiny shorts that left very little to the imagination and forced her to keep her eyes carefully averted.

She smiled warmly, fixing her eyes on a spot over David's shoulder rather than on the dark hair that dotted his exposed thighs. "I can't believe how many people turned up on such short notice."

"I can," he said with a huge smile that she caught out of the corner of her eye. "You're a magic worker, Bridget Moore."

"Anything for the animals," she said before Nichole grabbed her by the elbow and pulled her to the side.

"Wesley's here," she hissed into Bridget's ear. "Do you want me to tell him to get lost?"

Bridget followed Nichole's gaze until it landed on the newest arrival—a tall, lanky man with strong legs and white-blond hair. His eyes found hers, and for a moment it seemed as if everything around them fell away, as if no time had passed at all since that morning spent cooking together in his kitchen. But time had labored on, things had changed irreversibly.

He was here, but he was no longer *her* Wesley. He'd become a stranger—had always been one, now that she thought about it.

Then Nichole yanked on her arm again. "Well?"

"If he paid the fee, then he's welcome to run just like anyone else," she answered, forcing herself to look away from his intense gaze.

"You're far more forgiving than I'd be," Nichole grumbled, then headed off, presumably to share Bridget's decision with the others.

As soon as Nichole had gone, Wesley made his way over to Bridget. He looked the same as he always had, his eyes a warm, changeable blue like the sea rather than cold and dangerous. She still couldn't believe he'd committed a violent crime against a woman. Only the worst kinds of monsters did such things—at least that's what she had believed until recently.

Could Wesley still be good even though he'd done a bad thing?

She wished she knew, but the more she thought about it, the more muddled her opinions became.

He chanced a smile, his lips formed a circle, and she could tell he was ready to speak. Whether to offer an explanation or an apology, she didn't know. She also didn't want to find out.

This wasn't the right time. She had an event to oversee.

"Is everything okay?" Caleb asked after she'd charged up to him. As much as she hated herself for reverting to gender stereotypes, she felt safer with a man to keep her company rather than one of her female friends.

She wrapped her arms around herself in a hug. "Everything's good. I'm fine."

He tipped his chin in Wesley's direction. "Who's blondie over there?"

"Just someone I used to know."

His eyes narrowed as he regarded Wesley. "An ex-boyfriend—got it."

"No," she said, feeling a surge of sorrow in that instant. "We never got that far."

While Caleb waxed on about what he'd do to any guy that ever hurt his little sister, what he was willing to do today if she gave the word, Bridget mindlessly tapped around on her phone.

"Oh, it's time!" she cried. "I need to give the signal to start."

"Are you running?" her brother asked, leaning into a deep calf stretch.

"Yes, she is," Amy answered for her as she appeared out of nowhere. She held a megaphone that had been bedazzled with dozens of sparkly heart and animal stickers.

"Runners, take your places!" she cried way too close to Bridget's ear for comfort, then lowered the megaphone and pushed a bottle of water into Bridget's chest. "You're running. It'll be a good outlet for you."

"But I'm supposed to—"

"Already got it handled," she said, clicking the button on the handle of the megaphone demonstratively.

Caleb clapped a heavy hand on Bridget's shoulder, exchanging a conspiratorial smile with Amy. "Great. You're with me then, kid."

Bridget stared at both of them questioningly. It had never been in *her* plan to run, but obviously her happy helpers had gotten together behind her back to make a different decision.

"I'd get ready if I were you," Amy said sweetly before striding back to the position of honor right beside the line that marked both the start and the finish of their race.

"On your marks!" she cried.

Bridget twisted the cap from her water bottle and took a quick sip. Well, this was really happening. She'd never run without a dog at her side. She felt naked—vulnerable—without Teddy or Baby or Rosco.

"Get set!"

She searched the starting line until she found Wesley a few spots away.

"Go!"

She took off like a shot, running faster than she ever had. Amy and Caleb were right. She needed this.

Chapter 36

Bridget pumped her legs hard. The wind whipped the end of her ponytail against her cheek, but she brushed it aside and kept going full speed ahead. Even though she hadn't planned on running the race herself, she'd still worn sneakers and workout clothes as if somehow she'd known she would end up doing just that.

She followed the course laid out by Nichole, taking the first turn to the right—well ahead of most of the other runners, who were taking the race at a more leisurely pace. How nice it felt having a path that was already decided, to know that no matter the outcome, she'd done something good by organizing the race to support the shelter. If only the rest of her life could be like that. . . .

From Bridget's side, a familiar pale blur approached, then fell into step beside her.

Wesley.

"Are you finally going to talk to me?" she asked with a bitter laugh that drained her lungs, forcing her to slow her pace for the first time since Amy shouted *go*. She kept her eyes glued on the path, willing Wesley to pull ahead. He could run so much faster than she. He'd proven it many times.

"Because this really isn't a good time," she added with a slight growl when he refused to leave her side.

"I think it's the perfect time." Wesley wasn't winded in the slightest, which meant no matter how much faster she tried to go, he'd easily be able to keep up. That left her with two choices—turn back or listen to what he had to say.

Foolishly, perhaps, she chose the latter.

Bridget took another sip from her water bottle, then said, "You've got until the finish line. Speak."

She didn't look at him, only listened to his words over the sound of her wildly pumping heart. "I was wrong not to tell you," he began.

Bridget snorted in agreement. It had taken him long enough to realize that.

"It's not even that I didn't get the chance. You gave me so many openings. I'm sorry I didn't take them." His voice remained smooth, unlabored but not unfeeling.

"Why didn't you?" She chanced a look at him and found his expression to be soft, open. He wouldn't talk to her before, so why now?

Wesley licked his lips and continued. "I like you so much, Bridget. I tried not to, but the more I got to know you . . . *It's stupid.* I just didn't want to lose you, and I didn't want the way you look at me to change. Everyone else judges me based on my past. They never even get to know me before they decide to write me off altogether. But you, *you* kept coming back even when I was rude. You wanted something, so you made it happen, no matter what I did to try to stop you. I admire that so much." He said this last part with strange emphasis, almost as if he'd wanted to say something else but stopped himself before the words could make their debut.

"I don't know what you want me to say. You lied, kept a huge secret. If you like and *admire* me so much, why didn't you tell me and let me decide?" Maybe she was being unfair, but she'd have gone much easier on him if he'd come to her sooner. Time had only added to the sting of his betrayal. Did he know how much he'd hurt her? Had he been hurting, too?

He shook his head and stumbled slightly off course. "I know. I know. It's what I should have done, but I guess I'm a bit slow on the uptake. I haven't been out that long, and I'm still learning how to navigate this new life of mine."

"That's no excuse," she said stonily. This conversation would be so much easier if they focused only on the talking, but Wesley seemed to need the distraction of the race to open up to her at last.

They left the pavement and headed down a dirt trail that ran along the edge of the forest. The sun shone brightly overhead, beaming down on them as if it, too, wanted to be a part of their conversation. This felt far too familiar, far too comfortable. It would be so easy to fall back into their old patterns, but *easy* usually didn't mean *right*.

Bridget took another long pull from her water bottle, draining half of it in one go.

Wesley remained quiet, contemplative, for a couple minutes before finally speaking again. "I'm not here to make excuses. I came to apologize. Do you think you could ever forgive me?"

"I don't know," Bridget answered honestly. "I still don't know what you did, whether you're sorry for it, if I'm safe with you, or whether you'll keep big things from me again."

In short, she couldn't trust him. She'd found herself falling for him, trusting, maybe even beginning to love, but then the most fundamental requirement for a relationship had been torn right out from under her.

Without trust, could there be anything else?

"You're right," Wesley said, then exhaled deeply.

She turned toward him with a curious expression. Sometimes it felt as if he were right there inside Bridget's head with her.

"I shouldn't have kept such an important part of who I am from you, but I'm here now and ready to share. Just tell me what you would like to know. If you decide there's a way forward for us, I'll be so happy. If not, then I'll take it as a lesson learned. I like you so much, Bridget, but that doesn't mean you need to like me."

"Right now I don't like you very much," she admitted, and it was true. It was also not exactly true. *Stupid feelings.* "But I'll think about everything once I know everything. I can't make a decision with only part of the picture."

Wesley gulped hard. "You want to know what I did."

"I need to know." And in that moment, she knew he'd finally tell her. She only hoped she could live with the answer.

Chapter 37

The forest portion of the track ended, dumping them back onto the asphalt. Not a single cloud hung in the sky, allowing the sun to blaze directly onto the uncovered portions of Bridget's skin. Sweat beaded at her brow but merely threatened to fall rather than actually doing it. She'd finished her water now, and the heat had begun to wear on her.

Still, Bridget couldn't feel any sore or aching muscles. She didn't feel her lungs begging for oxygen, either. The only things that really mattered were Wesley and the words he was about to speak. She'd keep pressing forward. It's what she did, what she'd always done.

Wesley's normal pallor had been overtaken by a new pink, the sunburn forming right before her eyes as he struggled to explain the unexplainable. Because if it was easy, wouldn't he have shared this part of himself with her long ago?

"I'm not making excuses. Prison did change me," he said by way of an opening. "It made me rougher, more guarded, quicker to anger. Maybe I am dangerous as a result of having spent time there, though I would never hurt you, Bridget. I hope you believe me about that, even if you don't trust another word I say."

She nodded, not wanting to interrupt now that the moment of truth had finally arrived. Would she feel different once he'd revealed his past to her? Could his honesty now possibly be enough to make up for the fact that he'd hidden the truth from her for weeks and then disappeared from her life rather than so much as even attempting an explanation?

Not until today.

He ran an arm over his forehead to wipe the sweat from his hairline. "My best friend growing up was named Jon. My parents always worried he was a bad influence on me, but that didn't stop me from spending every free moment at his side. We got into all kinds of trouble as kids, but never anything serious."

Another pair of runners passed by them, and Wesley quieted until they were alone again.

"After we graduated, I went to college and he stayed home, supposedly working for his dad's construction business, though I doubt he ever worked an honest day in his life. I came back for Thanksgiving break my sophomore year, and Jon asked me to drive him to the gas station to pick up some snacks for the all-night gaming marathon we had planned."

Bridget's heart dropped as she realized where Wesley's story was headed. *No wonder he's so scared to let me in.*

Wesley bobbed his head as if answering a question she had not asked. "He never told me he planned to rob the place. I didn't even know he had a gun. I just sat there waiting outside the door like an idiot until Jon jumped in through the passenger door and told me to drive. He had a gun in one hand and the money in the other. Said he needed some extra cash to make Christmas happen this year. I think I may have heard the shot but wrote it off as a car backfiring. I never would have imagined . . ." His words trailed off. A haunted look overtook his eyes.

"That's awful," Bridget mumbled. She wanted to comfort

him, to protect him from his painful past—but it was too late. He'd already had to live with the outcome for years. It had changed the entire course of his life. She realized that now.

Wesley huffed and pumped his arms, taking a moment to focus on the run instead of his painful past.

"Then what happened?" she asked, scarcely above a whisper.

Wesley groaned. "Then of course he got caught, since his face was all over the security footage. I was there when he was arrested, when they told us that the clerk he'd shot was in critical condition at the local hospital. I felt so ashamed for ever having known him, for considering him a brother when he was capable of something so dark."

One thing still didn't make sense to Bridget. "How did you get involved, though?"

"I drove the getaway car," he said with a sad laugh. "And Jon wasted no time turning me in so that he could get a lighter sentence for himself. They had my plates, anyway, but Jon's testimony was what really sealed the case against me. He said I'd helped him plan the entire thing from start to finish, that I knew what was coming the whole time."

"But you had no idea." It wasn't a question. She'd known even before he'd told her about Jon today. Just by Wesley's willingness to share the truth, Bridget had understood his innocence. He'd made bad choices, but he hadn't hurt anyone, other than himself—and then, much later, her.

He was trying to make amends now, to secure her forgiveness. But could she give it?

Wesley inhaled sharply and risked a glance her way. "I had no idea, but the fact remained, I drove that car. I could've pushed him out and sped off without him, but I didn't. I took him back to his house, made an excuse, and left. I was sick to my stomach with fear, guilt, shame, the entire time, but I did it, and in that way I *am* guilty. I deserved what I got."

Bridget didn't know what to say, so she simply nodded and waited to see if Wesley would share more. Had he finished? And if he had, what did he expect from her now that he'd told her everything?

Too much of her brain was focused on propelling her body quickly toward the finish line, too much was thinking ahead to the activities that would happen after. She wanted to give Wesley her full attention, to have an answer for him now, but she just couldn't.

"Anyway," he said after a long pause. "Now you know."

He'd left her to wonder for weeks before finally turning up to explain himself. And now that it was her turn to speak, she, too, needed more time. . . . She hoped he'd be able to understand that.

Chapter 38

Despite their strong start, neither Bridget nor Wesley was among the top finishers for their group. Even so, her friends greeted her at the finish line with hugs, snacks, and a chorus line of *well dones*.

No one stood waiting for Wesley.

Bridget watched him return to his car while her loved ones prattled on. He didn't have anyone. His first great friend had betrayed him in almost the worst possible way, and he'd worked hard to keep others out since then. Wesley had let Bridget in, but only so far.

No wonder he was scared.

No wonder he hadn't wanted to reveal his sordid past and risk losing her so early in their relationship.

She hadn't liked what he'd done, but she also couldn't hold it against him. Not anymore.

Everyone laughed at something her father said, and Bridget joined in, too. She never took her eyes off Wesley, though—not until he came back, carrying a small slip of paper with him.

"Here's my donation for the shelter," he said with a determined smile as he placed the thin envelope in her hands.

"You know everything now. I don't deserve your forgiveness, and I don't expect it, either, but at least you know."

He left without another word.

Why did everything have to happen so fast all of a sudden? She needed time to process the new information, her new feelings.

"What was that all about?" Nichole asked, staring daggers after him.

"He apologized and told me the truth." She softened as she watched Wesley walk away from her the second time in the space of just a few minutes.

"Yeah, a bit late for that," Hazel added with a sarcastic snort.

"Are you okay?" Amy asked, her eyes searching Bridget's.

"I will be," she answered, knowing that one way or another, she would be. Wesley had given her the greatest gift of all—honesty—and it would lead to either a fresh beginning for them or closure for Bridget. The question was, *Which did she crave more?*

"Just forget about him," Hazel said. "This event was a huge success. I've already seen a few adoption applications come in, too!"

"That's great." Bridget hated that she had to force enthusiasm into her voice, but she was still in shock from Wesley's big revelation. If he'd just told her up-front, she could have easily forgiven him his past. After all, she understood being backed into a corner by someone you trusted—but the fact that he hadn't shared still made her wonder how much of his tale was true and how much of it had been recast to make him appear in a more favorable light. She couldn't picture him shooting anyone, but had he really not known Jon's plan?

She fingered the envelope in her hands. What was he doing making a donation, anyway? Her one visit to his apartment had made it readily apparent that he had very little and even less to spare. Could he really afford a gift to the charity? They'd already surpassed their fundraising goal. They didn't need it. She could return the check uncashed, not just to save him the expense but also to make sure he knew that her forgiveness couldn't be bought.

Her decision solidified when she finally opened the envelope and found a check for $2,500 waiting inside. The large sum burned hot in her hands. She couldn't accept this and would need to give it back. As soon as the event ended, she'd march straight up to his apartment and tell him that this was not okay.

"Bridget!" David cried, walking toward her while clapping slowly. He'd put on a pair of track pants since she'd last seen him, which made it easier for her to meet his eyes now. "Marvelous job! *Brava!*"

"Thanks," she responded shyly, tucking back a stray tendril that had worked itself loose from her ponytail. "It really was a team effort."

He *tsk*ed at her, but his enormous smile remained. "But you're the secret weapon. It seems you never run out of new ideas to help the animals here."

She felt a hot flush rise to her cheeks. "Oh, thank you. That means a lot." And it did. She loved helping the shelter, helping the animals, so why couldn't she focus on that? Why did her mind stay with Wesley even after he'd left?

David nodded, then glanced over his shoulder before turning back to Bridget. "Well, I'll let you get back to your friends. I have an important meeting to make, but I'll call you soon to wrap things up."

"Okay, bye!"

"He's kind of cute," Nichole said as the friends watched him walk away.

"Also really old and really married," Bridget said, barely containing her disgust. Today she'd seen way more of the committee head than she'd ever be able to erase from her brain. To think Nichole might actually want to see more? *Barf.*

"Hey, I was just looking. It's not like I even want a man in my life."

"You and me both," Bridget said with a giggle.

"You don't know what you're missing," Hazel chimed in, flashing her magnificent engagement ring around.

"I've got to agree with Hazel on this one," Amy said with an apologetic shrug.

Nichole looped an arm around Bridget's shoulders. "You two enjoy becoming 1950s housewives. Meanwhile Bridget and I will keep on having fun and living our best lives."

Bridget laughed and agreed heartily, but inside she knew something had changed. Wesley had made her realize how much more she could still add to her life without losing any of the things that already mattered.

And no matter what happened next, she'd forever be grateful to him.

Chapter 39

After the race, the girls took Bridget out for lunch at a steak-house to celebrate the event's huge success. Insisted on paying, too.

"How does it feel now that it's over?" Amy asked after everyone had toasted to Bridget.

"Like I'll probably have another one to plan very soon," she said with a sly smile.

"If that's true, then we might as well start now!" Nichole shouted.

"Hear, hear! This last-minute stuff is killing us," Hazel cried, and they all toasted again.

Bridget enjoyed the extra time with her friends, even though she knew she'd be seeing them all again tomorrow for the Sunday Potluck Club. They never skipped a week, no matter what else they had going on in their lives, and she liked that.

It was nice to know that this thing that had become so important to her was important to them, too. In a way, that's what she loved best, knowing she wasn't alone. No matter how hectic life got the other six days of the week, it would always slow to a crawl on Sundays.

Tragedy had brought them together, but their strength kept them that way. It would have been so easy for any one of them to give up after losing the important people in their lives to cancer, but none of them had yet. Whenever one of the friends faltered, the others were there to help her up, to lend a hand, a shoulder.

Bridget had offered help just as often as she'd received it, and that kept her strong, too. Knowing she could make a difference, that she could still be of use to the people she loved, meant that much more when her own world was spinning too fast on its axis.

She'd had a rough summer, but she'd also survived it. Now they just had Hazel and Keith's wedding to close out the season, and it would be back to school for Bridget, back to the way life had been before her mother's final bout with sickness, before she'd lost something so important.

Bridget wasn't the same person she'd been before, but maybe that was okay. She'd grown, learned more about herself than she'd ever dared to ask—and even though she hadn't quite figured out what she wanted to do about her relationship with Wesley, she knew it would come to her when she was ready.

Some things took too long. Others didn't last quite long enough. And sometimes it sucked, sometimes it hurt, but always it was okay.

Everything in its own time.

Because that's life.

When finally Bridget returned home that day, her dogs tackled her at the door, slathering kisses all over her arms and face. She spent a solid half hour or more wrestling with the two big dogs and playing tug with the Pomeranian, who was small of stature but big in attitude.

"C'mon, Teddy," she said, when she knew she couldn't delay her visit to Wesley any longer. The little dog panted merrily while she clipped the leash to his collar and they headed out the door.

She'd been to his apartment only once but remembered exactly where it was located at the base of the building's north staircase opposite the courtyard.

What would she say when she saw him? She still didn't know for sure but hoped the right words would come to her when she needed them.

She knocked and waited.

When Wesley didn't answer, she knocked again.

Beau and Snow didn't howl, as they had when she'd visited before. Did this mean they'd gone out? Or was he there but intentionally avoiding her now that he'd said his piece? Did he even want her forgiveness?

Now she wasn't so sure.

She knocked again, but that same eerie silence greeted her.

Wesley had given her his number, but her message was one she needed to deliver in person rather than over the phone.

She knocked one final time, and at last the door swung open.

"Hi. How can I help you?" asked a youngish woman wearing loose pajamas as she looked Bridget up and down suspiciously.

"Is Wesley here?" Bridget asked, trying to look around her. Wow, despite how sorry he'd claimed to be, he'd sure moved on fast. She hadn't even known he'd been dating, so it was especially surprising that he was living with someone. Could it be platonic? This young woman certainly didn't look like a relative.

"Who's Wesley?" the woman asked, scrunching up her features in confusion.

Bridget wrung her hands around the leash. "Um, he lives here."

"Oh!" The girl laughed and bent to pet Teddy. "He's the one who lived here before I moved in. Do you know him? I have some of his mail."

"What? He moved out?" This hadn't been what Bridget had expected, but it sure explained a lot.

"Well, I haven't seen him around," she said with a giggle, then stuck her hand out toward Bridget. "Hi, I'm Hailey. Are you one of my new neighbors?"

Bridget smiled even though what she really wanted to do was to run away screaming. Where was Wesley, and why had he left without saying goodbye?

She shook her head and forced herself to focus on the woman standing before her. "I'm Bridget. I live upstairs. Welcome to the building. How long have you been here?"

"Oh, about two weeks now. It's so nice to finally meet some of the neighbors," Hailey continued, flipping her sandy hair out of her face. "The brochures and website went on and on about how friendly and community based this place is, but you're the first one I've actually met."

Bridget smiled and reached into her pocket for her phone. "Then let me give you my number in case you ever need anything."

Hailey sighed with noticeable relief, then flashed a gigantic smile. "Oh, that's so nice. Come in. Come in!"

As the door closed behind Bridget, she felt as if something important had come to an end. Hailey seemed nice enough, but she wasn't Wesley.

Would never be Wesley.

Suddenly, Bridget knew the answer she'd been searching for all that day. She needed Wesley in her life. She'd always needed him.

Now she just had to find him and pray he felt the same way.

Chapter 40

Bridget returned to her apartment carrying the small bundle of Wesley's mail Hailey had entrusted to her. She still had his donation check, too. Even though Bridget preferred not to call, it seemed she had no other choice if she wanted to get in touch with him.

And she definitely wanted to.

After taking a deep, measured breath, Bridget leaned against the kitchen counter with a glass of water in one hand and her phone in the other. She hadn't actually ever called him before— not once—a fact that felt strange given how much time they'd once spent together.

When she called his number now, it delivered her straight to voice mail. She tried again and received a notice that the voice mail box was full. She texted and received a return message that the feature has been disabled on the account.

Darn it!

What now?

If she'd known the race would be her last chance to see him, she would have shared her feelings with him right then and there. She would have told him how confused she felt but then she'd have pushed through it and made a decision, anyway.

But she hadn't done that.

Instead, she'd let him walk right out of her life. *Again*.

"You miss him. Don't you?" Amy asked at their get-together the following day. The Potluck Club was meeting at Amy's that week, which meant she had no trouble pulling Bridget away from the others to speak with her privately.

Bridget shook her head and tried to arrange her features into a neutral mask. "I told Trent I'd stay away, so that's what I'm doing."

"Did Wesley talk to you at the event yesterday?" Amy wanted to know.

Bridget began to argue but then realized something wasn't quite right with this conversation. She kept the assurances she'd planned to offer her friend locked up tight inside and instead asked, "Wait, did you know he was going to do that?"

Amy bit her lip and nodded. "Yes. I mean, maybe. Just don't be mad, okay? I can tell how much you miss him, and it's kind of my fault things ended the way they did."

"You're not the one who sent him to jail or made him lie about it to me." Bridget wished she could tell Amy everything, but Wesley's secrets weren't hers to share. Even if she never saw him again, she'd respect that.

"Yeah, but I didn't help that confrontation between him and Trent, either. Trent couldn't remember what exactly he was in for, just that a woman had been attacked. When he checked, he found out that Wesley was charged as an accomplice in an armed robbery. Not as the actual guy who committed it, but as the getaway driver."

"Yeah, Wesley told me that." Hot tears pricked Bridget's eyes, but she couldn't let herself cry. If she did, Amy wouldn't let her get away without a long heart-to-heart, and the only heart Bridget needed to hear from right now was Wesley's.

"Does it change how you feel?" her friend asked softly.

"I don't know how I feel." *A necessary lie.*

"I do. I've known since you first mentioned running with him. I shouldn't have teased you so much about having a crush."

"A crush? Is that what it was?" Being with Wesley had felt like so much more. Calling it a *crush* relegated it to the halls of a middle school—a silly little thing. *Crush* didn't speak to how deep their feelings for each other had run beneath the surface. Of course, she felt crushed now that it was over. . . . Or was it?

"Only you know for sure. Do you want to forgive him?"

"He went to prison, Amy. That's not a small thing."

"I know," Amy said in that sweet way of hers. "But you're also not a small person. I've never known you to judge anyone, especially for things they can't necessarily control. He can't change his past. None of us can. What kind of person is he now?"

"One who lied to me. Or at least hid a big part of the truth." As they continued their discussion, it felt more and more as if Bridget were arguing with her own lingering insecurities and not Amy.

"Yeah, that was bad, but what else? I never got to know him, so I can't help here. What kind of man is he outside of this whole"—she swept her hand in a circle—"prison thing?"

Bridget laughed at her friend's choice of words. "Prison thing, huh?"

Amy just shrugged and waited. She wasn't often pushy, but once Amy decided something would help one of her friends, she refused to let it go.

Bridget sighed. "He did try to keep me away, said I didn't want a friend like him. And even though he didn't want me running with him at first, he saw that it was important to me and so he let me come. He was patient with me even though I slowed him way down on those first few runs. He taught me how to cook, made me laugh, and doted on my dogs. He even bought me a little stuffed dog that looks like Teddy just because."

Amy smiled. "Sounds like he was pretty great."

"Most of the time," Bridget admitted. "I still don't get it, though. If he'd just told me, I would have been okay with it. I would have been shocked and had a lot of questions, but I would have easily seen him for the man he is now rather than who he was then."

"Sometimes we hide things from those we care about in order to protect them. Maybe that's what Wesley was trying to do, as misguided as we now know that was."

"But I would never do something like that. I—" Bridget stopped abruptly. "I did exactly that by trying to keep the fundraiser from you guys, didn't I?"

Amy pointed at her and made a little clicking sound. "Bull's-eye."

"Okay, Ms. Smart Gal, you got me. So what should I do now?"

"Well, you still haven't answered my original question. Do you miss him?" Amy's gaze bored into her. Whatever Bridget answered now wouldn't matter; her friend would see the truth even if it didn't match her words.

Best not to lie. There had been too many lies already.

"Yes," Bridget confessed, realizing just how much truth that one tiny word held. "Yes, I do."

Amy hugged Bridget tight, then let go. "Then you know exactly what you need to do, but first let's go get some more cookies."

Chapter 41

Bridget had been sitting in the parking lot outside the small café for at least ten minutes already. She studied her face in her car's rearview mirror, stopping just short of whispering affirmations to herself. She'd already elicited a concerned glance from an elderly woman passing by.

Normally, she didn't care much what others thought of her or about how she looked, but today she agonized over both. Her clumpy mascara and overgrown eyebrows made her look like a tween only playing at the role of woman. She also spied a new pimple blossoming into existence near her hairline. She never got pimples, but of course she'd have one now that it actually mattered.

Her cell phone rang in the cupholder beside her—David from the shelter. She sent the call straight to voice mail and then silenced the ringer.

The last thing she needed was distractions. This would already be difficult enough without any extra help from the outside.

This was it. It was time.

The sign for Bailey's had been drawn in ornate, loopy script, a bit too fancy, given the family-friendly atmosphere inside. A little jingling bell announced her arrival as she pushed through the glass door and stepped in front of the hostess station.

It was two P.M. on a Monday, too late for the lunch rush and too early for dinner. She'd gotten special permission to leave the vet clinic early just so she could make this visit. Now fate would decide the rest, she supposed. Either Wesley was here and would agree to talk with her, or she'd have missed him yet again.

A heavyset middle-aged woman marched over with a stack of menus loaded in her arms. She smiled when she noticed Bridget waiting on the oversized welcome mat. "Hello, dear. Just one today?"

"Yes, please. But I'm hoping to make it two. Is Wesley here?" She glanced hopefully toward the little window that looked back into the kitchen but didn't see Wesley or anyone else behind it.

The waitress dropped the menus in the waiting rack, then studied Bridget a bit more closely, a huge grin lighting her face. "Oh, yes, he is. I'll send him straight out. Go ahead and pick any table you want. I'm sure he'll only be a minute."

Bridget thanked her, then found a small booth in the back corner of the restaurant. The tall seats made of worn leather would provide a nice private alcove where she and Wesley could speak freely—at least that's what she hoped.

Five minutes passed, then ten.

Hmm. The waitress had confirmed that Wesley was here, so why wasn't he *here*?

Another five minutes passed.

Was he just as nervous to meet with her as she was to see him again? Or maybe he was making a getaway while Bridget was otherwise occupied? Either seemed equally likely.

She'd begun to debate asking after Wesley again when at

last her former neighbor/friend/crush appeared carrying a mug of coffee for each of them along with a bowl full of disposable creamers.

The waitress from earlier scuttled over with two slices of warm apple pie, set them on the table, and rushed off with a swinging gait.

"Sorry about the wait," he said with a tight-lipped smile, almost as if he were afraid to assume anything positive could come from this interaction. "I needed to take care of a few quick things so that I could clock out for the day."

Bridget opened one creamer and two packets of sugar and dumped them into the mug before her. "Sorry to bother you at work," she said as she swirled the contents together with a shining silver spoon. "I didn't know how else to get in touch with you."

"I know," Wesley said, finally sliding onto the bench seat across from her. "Sorry about that. I didn't think you'd want to find me. Otherwise, I would have made sure to tell you I'd moved."

She reached into her purse and extracted the envelope that held his check. "I can't accept this," she said, pushing it across the table toward him. "It's too much."

He shook his head and crossed his arms over his chest. "I can afford it, and I want you and the animals to have it."

"But how, Wesley? I know money is tight for you, and that's okay. It's so generous that you wanted to make a donation, but—"

"I found a new apartment that costs three hundred less per month, and I gave up a few nonessentials. So it's totally fine. The shelter needs this money more than I do."

"Nonessentials? Like your phone?" she asked, eyes wide with disbelief. Why had he done this? Was it for her? "You didn't have to do that," she added, averting her gaze as heat rushed into her cheeks.

When she glanced back toward him, Wesley's eyes glistened like melting ice caps. He pushed the check back across the table. "Please keep it. *Please.*"

She could continue to fight with him, or she could move on to the next thing she wanted to say. And Bridget worried if she battled with him too long about the donation, Wesley would leave before the most important things were said. She smiled, swallowing back any further argument.

"Okay, thank you for this, and thank you for telling me about . . ." She glanced around the restaurant, not wanting to accidentally reveal Wesley's secret to his coworkers. "*Everything,*" she finished at last.

"I'm sorry it wasn't sooner." His hand flinched, and Bridget wondered if he wanted to reach out and take hers, if maybe she wanted that, too.

"I know. That's not why I'm here, though." Her heart sped to a wild canter, each beat a whisper reminding her what needed to happen next. Wesley had at last opened himself up to her at the race, and now she needed to return the favor.

I admire you so much, he'd said. But did he feel the same way she'd now realized she'd felt ever since that evening early in their relationship when he'd brought soup to her apartment?

She didn't know. And there was only one way to find out.

Wesley flinched and looked away. "Then why are you here?" he mumbled into his coffee.

Bridget had to tell him. She owed it to both of them.

Chapter 42

Bridget stabbed her fork into the slice of apple pie sitting before her, not because she was hungry but because she needed a moment to think about how she wanted to say what came next. The apple filling tasted shockingly sweet after the bitterness of the coffee, even with the two packets of sugar Bridget had added to make it palatable.

She considered her words carefully as she chewed.

Wesley picked up his fork but didn't make a move for his pie; instead he bounced it nervously between his fingers.

At last she swallowed and said, "I understand why you were afraid to tell me. I still wish you had, but I do understand."

He nodded and wrapped his hands around his mug.

"Have you seen Jon since it all happened?" she asked, wondering if she was prying. It wasn't that she needed to know, just that she needed him to understand she was still here, she was someone he could talk to.

Wesley frowned into his coffee. "Not since court. Even with his commuted sentence, he's still in for a lot longer than I was. Since he was the one to actually fire the gun, he got sent out of state to a max facility while I got to stay at Goose Creek, the same prison where your friend works as a guard."

She nodded along, making sure she kept her expression neutral. If he felt judged, Wesley would run—and they both knew she wouldn't have a prayer's chance of catching up to him again. "Have you forgiven him?" she asked thoughtfully.

"A long time ago. He made his choices, and I made mine. There isn't any going back, so we may as well move forward."

Bridget nodded again. "That's how I feel, too. I wish we could have started out differently, but what's done is done. Now that I know this huge, important thing about you, I feel like I understand you better, too."

"I'm not the same man I was then," he insisted as he set his fork down and laid his hands on the tabletop.

She reached out and took one in hers. "I know. Life has changed me a lot recently, too. Losing my mom . . ."

Bridget paused to avoid crying. "I'll never be the same, but it doesn't mean I have to settle for being anything less than I want to be. And neither do you."

"People judge me. I had to apply for more than two dozen jobs before I finally found someone who would say yes. Same with apartments. Nobody wants me around. Not with my record."

Before meeting Wesley that summer, Bridget would have been just the same as all those other people—unwilling to give him a chance when there were so many others out there who could fill a job, rent an apartment, be a friend.

But wasn't it the scars of life that gave a person character? Her best friends had all come together for just that reason: their hurts matched. Although their past struggles looked different, perhaps Wesley and Bridget could still fit together, too.

She wanted that and hoped he did, too.

"I do. I want you around." She let her words sink in,

those two little words that said so much, that said it all. "And if others judge you based on a past that you've already made up for, well, that's their loss. Me? I don't like losing, and I don't want to lose the friendship we've built. Lord knows you didn't make it easy."

They both laughed gently. Something broke between them—not a bond, but a wall. Now they sat face-to-face in full view of each other, with open minds, open hearts.

Bridget's look turned stern. "I get that you were trying to protect me by keeping me away, but I'm strong enough to protect myself. So don't ever do that again, okay?"

He let out a full, rich laugh now. "Okay."

"I forgive you for not telling me sooner, but that doesn't mean I won't get angry at you about something else, maybe about lots of something elses. We'll take each one as it comes, because that's what friends do."

Wesley appeared sad for a moment, then his face lifted in a warm grin. His icy exterior had also cracked and was finally letting the warmth inside shine through. "I haven't had a good friend in a long time, and before that I had Jon, who did more harm than good."

"Well, now you have me. And I'm not going anywhere unless you send me away again. You're so much more than just some guy who went to prison, Wesley. You have a kind and generous heart. Heck, even your dogs are proof of that." She reached into her bag and took out the gift she'd stashed inside. When planning for today, she hadn't been certain they'd reach this point. She'd hoped, though, and that's why she was ready now. . . .

"Boo," Wesley said upon spotting the plush Pomeranian he'd given her less than a month earlier. "The world's cutest dog. After Teddy, of course."

Bridget playfully walked the dog across the table and bumped him into Wesley's hand. "I know you meant this as a gift for me, but I want you to have it. That way you'll see him and know that I'm there for you, that you have at least one person in the world who sees past everything."

Wesley accepted the small toy and raised it to meet his eyes. "Do the dogs miss me?" he asked, keeping his eyes on Boo as he spoke.

"Not as much as I have, but they'll be happy to see you again for sure."

"What about your friends? What about Trent?"

"They'll be happy that I'm happy."

He frowned, but then Bridget reached for both of his hands and held them tightly in hers. "And I am. Happy, I mean."

"Me, too," he said, his voice cracking on that last word. "Me, too."

Chapter 43

Bridget and Wesley sat in that corner booth for a long time. He told her more of his back story, and she shared memories from her past, too.

"So you met all your Potluck Club friends in the cancer ward?" he asked, both eyebrows raised in surprise. Everyone reacted that way when they found out about the club's origins.

"More like in the hospital cafeteria, but yeah. Each of us had a parent going through treatment. We met Hazel last. Her father didn't stick around long before deciding he'd rather die on his own terms and in his own home." Bridget placed a final crease in her napkin, completing its transformation into an origami fortune teller.

When she was young they'd been called cootie catchers. All the other kids had stopped making them after fifth grade, but Bridget had continued to fold scraps of paper into the soothing pattern whenever the mood struck.

Choose a number. Discover your future.

"That must have been really hard on her," Wesley said, returning her squarely to the past. Such awful circumstances had brought her friends together, and yet another one had helped her to discover the true nature of her feelings for Wesley.

Bad came with good, if you stuck around long enough to find it.

Did Wesley know this, too?

Bridget swept her fortune teller to the side of the table. *Stop fidgeting*, she scolded herself.

"It was," she confided in Wesley now, "and it's why we decided to move our meetups outside of the hospital. That way Hazel could still be a part of it with us."

Wesley scooped up her craft project and tried to go through the motions, but the napkin was too weak to be further manipulated. He, too, swept it aside. "You were good friends to her."

"We're all always there for one another, no matter what."

He cleared his throat after choking on nothing. Why had her words surprised him? Was it because his friendships had turned out so differently?

She hated that. Wanted something different for him now. But she couldn't be the one to change the course of his life. He had to do that for himself.

Wesley sniffed and averted his gaze to his lap. "That's why they got so worried, when I showed up. They'll never accept—"

Bridget grabbed his hand and forced him to raise his eyes to meet hers. "No. *They will*. Trent didn't know the full story about how you were involved with what happened back then. It was the fact that I had no idea about your past that really set them into protective mode."

"I deserved that," he said morosely, but at least he didn't apologize again. He'd already mumbled a dozen different versions of "sorry" that afternoon, and if he couldn't move past it, then their friendship would be stuck right there. She so badly wanted to start over.

"Yes, you did, but you also deserve a second chance." Suddenly, Bridget had an idea that excited her, and she needed to share it with Wesley. "Come with me this weekend."

"Come where?" He pulled back slightly, caught off guard by her sudden change in demeanor.

Bridget squeezed his hand, willed him to read her heart as she tried to transmit her emotions through their skin-to-skin connection. "To Hazel and Keith's wedding. Be my plus-one."

"Are you sure they're ready for that?"

"I'll give them a heads-up. Amy is the one who encouraged me to find and talk to you, you know. I'm sure she's had a heart-to-heart with Trent, too."

He twisted his face in thought, ending on a frown. "But I don't have a nice suit."

"Come as you are. No judgment, seriously." Judgment was what had screwed them up before—his fear of it and her inability to avoid it.

"I'll feel weird if I'm the only one who's not dressed up, like everyone's staring at me."

"Then borrow a suit from my brother."

"But—"

"No more excuses. Please, do this for me. It will make everything so much easier. Plus, it wouldn't be a party without you."

A pink blush crept to Wesley's cheek, giving him a boyish charm. "Okay," he said with a nervous smile.

"*Okay*," she said, finally letting go of his hand. Before she could move her hand back to her side of the table, Wesley grabbed it again and gave her a meaningful look.

"How did I get so lucky to deserve a friend like you?" he asked, blue eyes shining with warmth, happiness.

"You don't," she answered with a playful laugh. "At least not yet, but keep working on it. I'm sure you'll get there someday."

He picked up her other hand and leaned forward in his seat. For one breathless moment, Bridget thought he might kiss her right then and there, right now in front of the growing dinner crowd.

Instead, he pulled each of her hands to his lips and kissed the backs of them. "That's exactly what I plan to do," he promised.

A thrill ran through Bridget as she giggled again. She'd never felt the touch of his lips before, but now she wanted to feel them again and again. Preferably pressed against hers.

What are you doing, Bridget?

She wasn't supposed to want him; she wasn't supposed to want anyone in that way. But maybe that's why they called it falling in love. Because once you were stumbling, it was already too late to pull yourself back on your feet.

This time with Wesley hadn't felt like a simple afternoon spent with a friend, a mere reconciliation. Instead, it had felt as if maybe it could be the beginning of forever.

Chapter 44

Bridget fought against the hair straightener as she attempted to take the frizz out of her long dark hair. Instead, her efforts just seemed to be making everything worse. Hazel had arranged salon appointments for all the members of her bridal party, but when one of the stylists called in sick at the last minute, Bridget and Nichole had both volunteered to work on their own hair.

She had since started to regret that decision.

Of course no one would be looking at her next to gorgeous Hazel in full bridal accoutrement. . . . Well, no one except Wesley.

Her heart leaped into her throat, forcing her to swallow repeatedly so she could breathe.

She needed to stop thinking of him like this, at least for now. They'd only just become friends again. Adding romantic feelings to the mix would make everything that much more difficult.

Then again, could she really choose how she felt?

It sure didn't seem that way. Otherwise she'd already have moved past the grief of losing her mother. She'd think of Wesley in strictly platonic terms and be the friend he needed to help him reenter a world that had turned its back on the poor guy a long time ago.

No, Bridget had no control over her stupid heart at all. Nor her schedule, it seemed, as her phone buzzed with a string of incoming texts from Amy:

The dove has left the nest.

I repeat, the dove has left the nest!

Let's do this thing!

They still had a couple hours until go time, but everyone had agreed to meet at the church early since Bridget and Nichole had skipped the salon. So much time had passed, and still Bridget's hair wasn't even close to presentable. Maybe Amy or Nichole would be able to help her finish getting ready once they were all together—or maybe she could just pull it back into a tight ponytail and be done with it.

On my way! she texted back along with a goofy selfie that showed just how very not ready she was.

And her phone lit up with a call almost immediately after she pressed Send.

"Bring hairspray, bobby pins, a brush, whatever you've got to help tame that nest on your head." Amy hung up before Bridget could verbalize a response. It looked like Bridget and her hair would be getting help, after all.

It was almost time.

Bridget couldn't help but peek through the small window near the top of the door, and what she saw waiting inside simply took her breath away.

Beautiful garlands of orange poppies lined both sides of the church aisle. Guests filled the twin lines of pews inside the small church, and some folks even had to stand at the back for lack of space to accommodate them all.

The church looked so different today than it had for the

funeral more than one year ago. Yes, Hazel was getting married in the same church she had attended as a girl, the same church that had hosted her father's big send-off to Heaven.

That was why not a single white flower graced the building. It had already seen enough ethereal, peaceful white from the Long family. Hazel had declared her wedding would be a joyous festivity, and what happier color than orange?

Bridget glanced down at her bouquet of poppies mixed in with Asiatic lilies and English roses, a lovely arrangement of both bright and soothing oranges. Beautiful. Just like the bride herself.

Would Bridget find herself in Hazel's place one day?

For the first time, she wanted this.

She wanted everything life had to offer. No more rushing through each day, praying that things would get better eventually. She would make things happen and enjoy them when they did.

Because now she realized what she should've known all along: life was defined by the people you let in. Her mother, her friends, and even her dogs—for animals were people, too—together, they formed the very foundation of her world. They had shaped her into the person she'd become, the person she would one day be.

Why had she been so insistent on keeping new people out? So she could stay busy and hide from her feelings? She'd gotten it all so horribly wrong. Her loved ones would help her heal, not busy work. It didn't matter how noble her efforts or how ambitious her goals when she was using them as a way to forget love.

Hiding from her mother's memory meant hiding from a huge part of her heart. No wonder she'd felt so beaten down. And she'd spent weeks hiding from her feelings for Wesley, too.

Well, no more.

"Are you ready to do this?" she asked her friend with one last glance toward the waiting crowd. Yes, Bridget was ready not only for the wedding but also for what came next for herself.

Hazel nodded and hooked an arm through Bridget's. Amy took Hazel's other arm, and Nichole latched onto Bridget's free side.

The church aisle was spacious, wide enough to allow the four friends to walk side by side as the members of the Sunday Potluck Club gave away one of their own to the lucky man who had won her heart.

Hazel didn't have her father anymore, but he had led her to these great friends and to an even greater love during his final weeks of life. Bridget found that beautiful.

And, yes, she cried as the four of them walked toward Hazel's future, arm in arm amidst a floral sunset.

In a world that had given them so may endings, finally there was a new beginning to celebrate. And Bridget knew in her heart that this would be the first of many.

Life didn't stop if a person became too afraid to live it.

Bridget needed to stop being afraid of what might happen and enjoy everything that already had. As she watched Hazel and Keith exchange vows, she made this promise to herself.

No more racing through life.

It was time to enjoy the journey.

Chapter 45

When Bridget reached the reception hall, she found Wesley seated by himself at a table up-front. He wore a pale-blue buttoned shirt and black pants, both of which suited him perfectly despite his earlier worry.

"I'll be right back," she told Nichole as she broke away from the rest of the bridal party.

Wesley noticed her when she was just a few paces away. He stood abruptly and stuck both hands in his pockets. "You look nice," he mumbled as she closed the rest of the distance between them.

"Just nice? I'll have you know I put a lot of effort into this look, and just nice isn't going to cut it." She giggled and placed a hand on his upper chest. Bridget had never been the flirtatious type before, but she couldn't bear the thought of this evening coming to an end without Wesley knowing exactly how she felt.

That was the promise she had made to herself at the altar, and she intended to keep it.

Wesley swallowed hard as he took in Bridget's gown, hair, and makeup. "Stunningly beautiful," he murmured.

"That's better." She pulled his hands out of his pockets so that he could return the hug she gave him next. "Did you catch the ceremony? I didn't see you there."

"No," he whispered, loosening his hold on Bridget. "I didn't want to ruin their special day."

She stepped back and narrowed her eyes at Wesley, searching. His eyes kept no secrets—not anymore—and right now they were telling her just how uncomfortable he felt, here among her friends.

And even with Bridget herself.

"This ends now," she said. They'd lost enough time hiding from the truths of their pasts and their feelings for each other, and Bridget refused to waste any more. Today was about new beginnings, about celebrating all the best parts of life.

"What?" Wesley asked as she jerked him away from the table and dragged him over to her friends, who still stood waiting near the doorway.

Hazel and Keith hadn't made it into the reception hall yet, but their many guests had gathered in a crowd to wait for their grand arrival. Bridget approached Nichole first. "Nic, you remember Wesley. Right? He's my plus-one for the night."

"Hi," her friend said, twiddling her fingers in a casual wave.

Next Bridget turned to Amy and Trent. "Wesley is my plus-one tonight. He'll be sitting at our table, too, so I figured we should get any awkwardness out of the way early."

Amy threw her arms around Wesley and hugged him tight. "I'm so glad you came!" she said, rocking him from side to side.

When she let go, Trent clamped a hand on Wesley's shoulder and offered the other in a firm handshake. "I'm all for starting over, if you are."

Wesley cleared his throat and tried to smile, but his discomfort remained obvious. "Yeah. I mean, yes. Please. That would be great."

Trent's daughter, Olivia, tugged on her father's hand. "Let's go dance, Daddy," she cried, already pulling him toward the DJ booth.

"But we're supposed to wait for the bride and groom to kick things off with the first dance," Trent argued as he remained rooted to the spot.

"I think an exception can be made for our flower girl," Amy countered, giving her boyfriend a gentle push. "Just make sure you save a dance for me, too!"

"He's such a good father," Nichole said as everyone watched Trent and Olivia take their places on the dance floor.

Amy nodded. "It's one of the things I love most about him."

Bridget could see Wesley tensing up again, so she wedged each of her fingers between his and pulled him in to her side. "Trent wouldn't have said that if he didn't mean it," she whispered in the direction of his ear. She was too short to whisper directly into it, which meant Amy overheard every word.

Her friend bobbed her head enthusiastically. The tight blond curls composing her elaborate half-up and half-down hairdo bounced like happy little springs. "Oh, yes. We all just want B to be happy, and we all see now that being with you makes her happier than we've ever seen her."

Wesley blushed. "Oh, no. We're not . . . I mean, she's not *with me.*"

Amy tilted her head toward Bridget and raised one eyebrow. "Well, perhaps she should be."

Bridget glanced up at Wesley. She'd had the same thought many times before but hadn't known how to broach the subject with him. Leave it to her friends to make the big move for her.

Wesley glanced down at Bridget and licked his lips. His shoulders heaved as he sucked in a deep breath, and his eyes danced with a secret that he promised to reveal soon. Would he confess that his heart matched the feeling in hers? Would he fight for her the way she wanted to fight for him?

This was it. Finally Bridget would have her answer.

A day for new beginnings . . .

A day for declaring love . . .

Making promises . . .

Wesley took a small step closer. "Bridget, I—"

Of course, this was the exact moment Hazel and Keith burst through the door to the roaring cheers of their guests.

Even though her moment had been delayed, Bridget refused to believe it was ruined, which meant, of course, that she cheered the loudest.

Chapter 46

A week had passed since Hazel and Keith's wedding.

Bridget hadn't found the right moment to share her feelings with Wesley that night, but they both knew it was coming. The way he looked at her ever since that night, the way his eyes danced and his lips curved up in a smile. . . .

And even though Wesley had moved to a different apartment complex, he came to meet Bridget in the courtyard every evening. They ran together with their dogs, then made dinner side by side in Bridget's kitchen. After they ate, he'd usually head home. Although there was one time when she convinced him to cuddle on the couch with her and watch the pilot episode of her all-time favorite show on Netflix.

Still no kiss.

Still no sweeping declarations of love.

Yes, Amy had broken the ice, but the wedding festivities had kept everyone so busy that their opportunity had frozen over yet again. And while Bridget wanted to have that talk with him, she'd built it up so much in her mind that she knew nothing less than perfect would do.

A part of her hoped he would declare his feelings first, but she also understood just how afraid he must be to ask for anything more than the second chance she'd already given him.

The past week had been wonderful, anyway.

She and Wesley had long talks, keeping nothing from each other this time around—well, nothing besides putting words to what was in their hearts. And whenever Bridget thought she felt Wesley backing away, she simply grabbed his hand, made him look into her eyes, and waited for him to come back to her.

She cared for him in a way she hadn't cared for anyone else in her life. Maybe part of it was knowing just how much he needed her, but in truth, she needed him every bit as much. Where she was soft, he was hard. He chose to do a few things well, whereas she liked to try everything that crossed her path. In that way, they made each other better. He brought her back down to earth, kept her grounded, while she encouraged him to reach for the stars. At least that's what she liked to think would happen whenever they finally changed their routine and got into the wide open world a bit more often.

For now, she was more than content in the happy little cocoon they'd built somewhere between friends and so much more.

That Saturday would be the first they hadn't seen each other since the wedding. Wesley had picked up a double shift at the restaurant, and Bridget had urged him to rest up and meet her for Potluck Club on Sunday if he could. Besides, she had her volunteer day at the shelter, and thanks to the timing of Hazel and Keith's wedding, she hadn't been in since the big fundraiser. She couldn't wait to hear how things had gone on the adoption front.

When she arrived at the facility, she found David waiting for her at reception. "You're a very tricky person to get ahold of," he said with an expression she found difficult to interpret.

"Really? Well, I had a wedding last Saturday, but other than that . . ."

David shook his head. "I tried calling a few times, too."

"Sorry," she said, heat rising to her cheeks. "I was always at work or running and forgot to call back. What's up?"

"Let's leash up some of the dogs and take a walk." His tone was just as indecipherable as his face.

Was Bridget in trouble? Had something gone wrong?

She followed David into the back kennels and chose a pit bull that reminded her of her own Baby. David leashed up a shepherd mix, and together they exited into the warm late-summer day. It seemed David had a lot on his mind, so Bridget refrained from asking any questions, instead waiting for him to say whatever he had asked her out here to say.

If it really was as bad as she feared, then someone would have told her by now. Right?

David frowned but remained silent until they rounded a copse of pines.

"We let May go," he said at last. "Turns out she was lying about a lot more than her involvement in the fundraiser."

"I'm sorry." Bridget felt horribly guilty, of course. As much as she disliked May, she hadn't meant to cost the woman her job.

"Don't be." David smiled toward the sun before returning his gaze to Bridget. "She was never right for the job, but luckily the board has the perfect person in mind to replace her."

This was surprising news. Had they brought someone in from the outside? Well, anyone would be better than May, if she were being honest with herself.

"Oh, who?" she asked, only vaguely interested at this point.

David's grin took over the whole lower half of his face. *"You."*

"What?" She stumbled on the path, which sent her heart galloping. Surely, she must be hearing things. David knew she couldn't afford to volunteer more than one day a week, especially with school starting up again.

If David sensed her hesitation, he did a good job of disguising it. "We want to offer you a full-time position with the shelter. That should make it easier for you to keep planning your brilliant events. Nobody loves these animals like you do. And they need you in their corner all week, not just Saturdays."

Bridget's face fell. Oh, no. She'd cost May her job, and now she'd need to leave the shelter just when they needed her most. "But I go back to school next week, and I work full-time at the veterinary clinic," she tried to explain gently.

David stopped walking and bent to pet the dogs they'd brought with them. "Devoting your life to a nonprofit isn't the most lucrative career path, but it *is* the most rewarding. I'm not asking to hire you for a little while or until something better comes along. I'm asking you to make this your path. It suits you, Bridget."

"Oh, wow, that's a lot to think about." How could she say no? But also how could she say yes? Bridget's life was already too full. There wasn't any space left.

"Promise me you'll consider my offer," David said before resuming their stroll.

She nodded her agreement, all the while knowing that it just couldn't work, not with everything else she'd already committed to. She hoped that David wouldn't be too disappointed when she was forced to turn down his kind offer.

Chapter 47

Bridget pulled her car into the lot nearest to the student union. Today was the first day of the new semester and her first day back since she'd taken an extended leave to watch over her sick mother. Exiting her car now felt like stepping out of a time machine and into a simpler past—one where her path had been straight, narrow, and clearly lit. She remembered those days when her mom had been in remission and they all thought she would live a full, long life.

But it was also a time when she hadn't yet met her best friends or Wesley. Before she'd started volunteering at the shelter. Before she'd become the Bridget she was today.

She liked this new Bridget, but that didn't mean she couldn't like the one she'd been before, too. Some aspects of life weren't as easy to pack into boxes and tuck away.

Out of sight but never quite out of mind.

No matter how busy she tried to stay, eventually life's hurts would find her and force her to confront them. There was no running from them, either. The only way out was through.

She knew that now, and she wanted to make sure Wesley knew it, too. That's why she had invited him here today. It wasn't just the first day of a new school year. It would be the official start of several things more, and she couldn't wait to share them with her friends.

But first . . .

Wesley spotted her before she saw him. "Bridget, over here!" he called, raising an arm to motion her over.

She grabbed the old tattered backpack from her trunk and jogged over to join him. "Hey. Thanks for meeting me here." As much as she wanted to appear casual, she could barely contain the excitement that bubbled inside.

So much had happened over the long Labor Day weekend—most of it inside her head—and now today was the day she'd officially bring the realizations she'd made to light.

Today was the first day of yet another new Bridget.

A better Bridget.

A Bridget who knew exactly where she was going, because she was already halfway there.

"What's up?" Wesley asked, raking a hand through his hair as he glanced around the campus, taking in the rush of students and faculty as they passed.

"It's the first day of the new term," she informed him plainly.

"Are you excited to be returning to school after all this time?" he asked as they fell into step beside each other and walked past the student union.

"I'm not," she told him, plopping down on the grass beneath a large tree and patting the ground for him to join her. "I mean I am excited, but I'm *not* returning."

Wesley's white-blond brows pinched in confusion, just as she'd suspected they would. "I don't get it. I thought you still had a year and a half left of undergrad and then four more years for your DVM. Did you decide to take more time off?"

She handed him the backpack once he'd settled down beside her on the ground. "I'm going to finish my bachelor of science by taking online and night classes. My new employer actually volunteered to pay for that."

He let out a low, impressed whistle. "Bridget, that's great! Which vet are you working at now?"

"I'm not," she said again. This was it. She could finally tell him the solution she'd spent the last several days puzzling out. "Actually, I've decided not to pursue veterinary school after all."

"I don't understand." He frowned, but when he found that she was smiling, he met her halfway with something of an optimistic grimace.

"Unzip that backpack and look inside." Excitement buzzed inside her as she waited for Wesley to connect all the pieces. Just as she had while lying awake in bed and contemplating the course of her life a couple nights ago.

He pulled out a stack of folders and notebooks, a box of pens, and last the cell phone she'd already activated and had charged to 100 percent on her drive over. Wesley laughed. "What is all this?"

She shook her head, refusing to tell him. She wanted him to see for himself. Needed him to.

"Check out the contacts on the phone," she nudged.

Wesley thumbed through the phone's various menus until he found what he was looking for. "There's only one." He clicked again. "Bridget Moore, and there's a number I don't recognize. Hey, it also says you're the Community Coordinator for the shelter."

He dropped the phone to his lap and gaped at her. "Seriously? That's wonderful! Congratulations!"

"They gave me a new phone to go with the job, and I figured you might be able to make use of my old one. We can get it officially transferred to your name after we're done here."

He looked at her in quiet awe.

"Well, don't just sit there staring at me. Bring it in for a hug," she cried, then reveled in the feeling of his strong arms around her.

"So that's why you're not going back to school?" he asked a few moments later.

"Pretty much."

He glanced toward the student union, idly watching all the people come and go. "Then why are we here?"

"Because *you're* going back, Wesley," she revealed. No, she hadn't decided for him. The choice would be Wesley's and Wesley's alone, but she needed him to know that new paths were open to him, too. That it wasn't too late to find the life he wanted and to make it his.

"What? How is that even possible?" He gasped in shock more than elation. That was okay. Bridget could be happy enough for both of them—at least to start.

"Well, it's not," she said gently. "At least not for this semester, but the school has all your old transcripts on file, and there are lots of scholarships out there to help ex-cons pay for school. You don't have to study engineering this time, either. You could get your culinary degree. Or really study anything. Absolutely anything you want. It's never too late to change your life. Just look at me!"

"Yes, just look at you," Wesley said, looping an arm over her shoulder and pulling her close. "I don't think I can stop."

Chapter 48

Bridget stood at Wesley's side while he talked with an admissions counselor, and she stayed there while he was loaded up with various brochures, catalogs, and pamphlets. He was still afraid of rewinding his life and going back to the place he'd been when everything had gone so terribly wrong; his nervous stutter made that obvious.

But he was willing to give it a chance, and that meant everything.

After all, Bridget was scared, too.

A life lived without fear, regrets, challenges wasn't really a life at all. She knew that now and had no doubt Wesley soon would as well.

"You sure have a lot to think about," she told him later as they headed back to the parking lot together.

Wesley smiled as he looked back over his shoulder toward the main campus. "Yeah, but I think I may already have the first steps figured out."

"Oh?" She looped her arm through his, eager to hear what he had decided.

He'd remained quiet while the admissions counselor spoke

at length. Had he been secretly working out a plan that whole time?

"Yeah, I'll tell you over dinner," he answered now with a sly grin. "First there's something we need to do."

She stared at him with an open smirk. *Such a tease.*

He chuckled at her. "Hey, you think you're the only one who can make big decisions about my life?"

"I saw something I knew could help you, so I pushed you in that direction. The decision is still yours."

"Oh, really? Well, remember that in about an hour, okay? Because I'm about to do the same thing for you."

Sure enough, when they returned to Bridget's apartment, Wesley said a quick hello to Teddy, Rosco, and Baby, then put both hands on his hips as he surveyed the living room. "Where is it?" he asked her.

"Where's what?"

"Your mother's box."

Immediately her stomach churned. Did they really need to do this today? She'd already worked through so much. And she would get to the box—*she would*—but first she needed to rest and celebrate. First she wanted to share her feelings with Wesley before revisiting the most painful part of her past.

"C'mon, out with it already," Wesley insisted. "You've told me more than once how this thing keeps you anchored to your grief. Well, my dear Bridget, it's time to finally set sail."

"Your *dear* Bridget?" she teased, his silly mood lightening the heaviness of the moment. She needed to do this, and it would help to have a good friend by her side.

"Under the bathroom sink," she told him with a defeated sigh.

She needed to face the contents of the box. It wouldn't be easy, but she'd survive.

Wesley went to retrieve it while Bridget picked up Teddy

and snuggled him close. Her mother had loved and petted this very same dog, and in that small way they were still connected. Her mother had seen the world as she'd once seen it, but things looked different now.

Perhaps a bit brighter.

Wesley reverently placed the cardboard box on her kitchen table, then took Teddy into his arms. "Remember, this is your decision."

She nodded. They hadn't spoken much about the box, but that didn't mean he hadn't picked up on the importance of the few words they had shared.

"Are you ready?" he asked, studying her carefully.

Bridget nodded. Perhaps a tear or two fell—she couldn't really say.

Everything she had went into pulling apart those nestled cardboard flaps and willing herself to lift the items out and consider them one by one.

The first thing she found was her baby blanket, which felt just as soft as the day she'd tucked it away in this cardboard prison. She found the scrapbook her friends had put together with her at the funeral after-party. Nichole had called it a hot mess because the photos had been cut and pasted at random with no rhyme or reason to their placement, but Bridget found the layout refreshingly spontaneous.

Just like her mother.

Just like life.

"She was gorgeous," Wesley said, resting his chin on Bridget's shoulder as she flipped through the pages. "And you look so much like her."

Bridget turned to him, the scrapbook still clutched to her chest as she cried softly into Wesley's shirt. "She was such a big part of my world."

"She can still be. Every time you do something wonderful, that's her living on through you."

This time Bridget knew for a fact she was crying. She couldn't help it, not when Wesley knew just what to say to comfort her, to help her get through what she'd put off for so long. Did that mean he had planned this moment the same way she'd planned the one at the college?

"What about when I do something stupid?" she asked with a sniff.

"Then, too." Wesley kissed the top of her head and chuckled. "Especially then, I bet."

"What about when I do this?" She placed a hand on each side of his chest and raised her face so she could see his better.

Wesley's eyes flashed a bright, alluring blue. He parted his lips and let out one shaky breath. "Do what?" he asked with a teasing smile.

Bridget closed her eyes and pushed onto her tiptoes.

Waiting. Needing.

Finally, finally Wesley closed the rest of the distance between them, touching his lips to hers. It didn't feel like a first kiss—not to Bridget.

It felt like a forever kiss. The kind she and Wesley would share a million times in the years that followed, the one they'd share at the wedding altar one day, the one they'd have after welcoming their first child into the world, the one they'd give each other every day for the rest of their lives.

Yes, they'd both been beaten down by life, but they'd also both risen again, stood on unsure legs, and dared to journey forward.

And now, here they were doing it again.

Together.

Chapter 49

Bridget and Wesley finished unpacking her mother's box, taking frequent breaks to share a memory or exchange a quick kiss. Interspersing her future happiness with her past pain felt strangely perfect, as if it was always supposed to end up this way.

Only one item remained in the box now. It was the smallest but also the scariest.

Bridget pulled out the simple lined notepad; a list had been scrawled onto three of its pages. And the entire first page of that list had been completed with proud inked check marks to claim the triumphs of counting the stars, watching a sunrise on the beach, and more.

She turned the page and continued to read until the check marks disappeared. The next item—the one that read *run a charity race*—had been left in a permanent state of waiting.

But no.

They'd done that already, she and Wesley had. They'd run the charity race she'd organized for the shelter; it was the same day he'd confessed the truth to her, the same day she started on the road to forgiveness.

"Can you grab me a pen from the drawer under the

microwave?" she asked. Her mother had meant for them to do it together, but instead Bridget had done it for her. Just as Wesley had pointed out earlier, the mother's spirit and ambitions continued to live through her daughter.

When Wesley returned with a pen, she uncapped it and added its blue to the column of black checks.

"What's next?" he asked, cuddling her from behind.

"Swim with the dolphins," she read with a chuckle. "I don't know if she ever expected to do that one."

Wesley took the notebook from her hands. "Maybe she didn't expect to do it herself. Maybe she left it there for you."

A part of her wanted to believe, but she had to be careful about getting her hopes up. Her mother was gone and they had their memories, but it was too much to expect something new. Because that could very well break her heart.

Bridget shrugged. "*Maybe*. It seems like a very Mom thing to do."

"What else is on the list? Have you looked?"

"Actually, I haven't. Mom was very insistent that we do the list together and in order. She kept it in her nightstand and never showed me what else she'd written down."

"Show me."

She swallowed hard as the notebook passed from her hands to his.

Immediately Wesley turned the page and began to read from farther down the list.

"Eat at a Michelin-starred restaurant. Be an extra in a movie. Start a club. Visit each of the fifty states." He glanced up at her. "Bridget, this wasn't a list for her. It was meant for you."

She grabbed the notepad back, her eyes zooming right to the very bottom of that bulleted list. "Fall in love. Get married. Live a beautiful life," she read aloud, a fresh sheen of tears making it difficult to read anything else.

Her mother hadn't abandoned Bridget. She'd left clear instructions—simple instructions on how to live life without her. And Bridget had foolishly been too afraid to look.

That was, until Wesley directed her gaze right where it needed to be.

She picked the blue ink pen back off the table and placed a check next to *Fall in love*. Enough waiting for the perfect moment. Life happened whether or not you were ready for it, and she needed Wesley to know how much this afternoon had meant to her, how much he meant to her.

"Okay, what's next?" she asked, almost afraid to meet his eyes.

He drew close and placed strong hands on either side of her waist. "I know she left this list for you, but I'd like to be right there with you if you'll have me. I love you, too, Bridget. So much it scares me. You gave me back to myself. Nobody else could do that but you, Bridget."

She laughed through her tears as Wesley used the pad of his thumb to wipe them away. "Why didn't you tell me?"

"Didn't you know?"

She hit him playfully.

"Well, there's your answer," he said. "Kissing me one second, hitting me the next. I just never know with you."

She hit him again, but he grabbed her tight and pulled her in for a kiss.

"I much prefer the kissing, by the way."

Bridget stared into his soothing ocean eyes. She'd once thought of them as ice. This same man who held her now had once avoided her, insulted her, pushed her away at every opportunity.

How funny life could be.

Good thing Bridget had always had a pretty good sense of humor.

"Let's do it," she said. "Let's finish the list."

"A lot of the items on there are quite pricey. We'll have to save up."

"Luckily, we've got time."

Chapter 50

Bridget spent the next few weeks easing into her new job—her new *career*—as community outreach coordinator for the local animal shelter. It didn't take long for her to confirm that she'd made the right decision. Life experience did that; it taught you how to figure out what you needed and to make sure you got it.

Like Wesley.

She'd been so sure she hadn't wanted love, but really her entire world now revolved around it. Same as it always had.

Love for her mother, her father and brothers, her friends, the animals at the shelter, and—yes—even for herself.

Funny how a chance encounter with a rude stranger had set her on the exact path she needed to tread.

Wesley, too, had been keeping busy that month. He convinced his manager at the restaurant to grant him an extra shift each week, and even though he didn't have much to spend, he saved the added pay in a special cookie jar guarded by an adorable stuffed Pomeranian dressed as a lion. He and Bridget had taken to calling it the bucket, because someday it would finance the next item on her mother's list . . . and the next.

He took his extra-long work hours in stride, soaking up the experience and learning all he could. He'd already begun to prepare his applications to culinary school. One day he would have a restaurant of his own, and even if that day was still very far away, Bridget knew she'd be right there at his side to celebrate.

Next month would bring Halloween and Bridget's next big shelter event. With more time to prepare, she was able to dream bigger, reach further. The city council had already agreed to allow a pet parade for that afternoon, and Bridget was having the best time finding costumes to show off each dog's unique personality. After the parade, they'd host a Tricks and Treats party back at the shelter to drive adoptions and provide a fun, family-friendly alternative to trick-or-treating.

She was secretly praying for rain, knowing it would bring in even more families to visit the animals, that some would fall in love. Yes, sometimes all it took was looking in the right direction—or inside the right box—for everything to change for the better. Sometimes a little rain had to fall for something new to grow.

And the *something new* things kept right on coming for Bridget.

"Think anyone will show up?" she asked Wesley as they stood together in the courtyard.

Teddy barked happily in response. Teddy always barked about everything, though.

"Well?" She bumped her shoulder into Wesley's.

"Why so nervous?" he teased while Beau and Snow thumped their tails against the lawn. "You know it's going to be great."

"Do I?"

"Well, I do." He gave her a quick peck, and then a much longer, much tastier kiss.

"My eyes!" Nichole cried, drawing a hand over her face as if she'd been blinded. "Why are there kissing people wherever I look these days?"

"Oh, stop," Amy called as she, Trent, and Olivia arrived from the opposite side. They'd also brought Amy's beagle, Darwin, and Trent's black Lab, Jet, with them.

"I kind of feel naked without a dog at my side," Nichole said with a laugh.

"If I'd known you were coming, I'd have lent you Baby and Rosco," Bridget offered with a shrug.

"How could you not know?" Amy asked. "We wouldn't miss it for the world."

"It's not like this is a big shelter event. It's just the first meeting of the complex's newly revived walking club. A complex in which none of you live, by the way," she scolded, although secretly she was happy her friends had turned up to support her yet again.

Hazel appeared hand in hand with her new husband, Keith. "Yeah, but with you planning it, Wednesday Walks and Wags is sure to be the best walking club Alaska's ever seen."

"I'll drink to that," Trent said, raising a metal water bottle toward Bridget before taking a giant swig.

"That better be water in there!" she cried.

"Hello. Is this the new walking club?" a woman asked as she shyly approached the large group of friends. She seemed familiar, although Bridget couldn't quite place her.

Bridget rushed forward to greet her. "Yes, welcome!"

"Bridget? I had no idea you'd be leading it. Cool."

That's when she remembered. "Hey, Wesley. I'd like you to meet Hailey, the new tenant in your old apartment."

They exchanged hellos as a few more neighbors arrived to join the club, some with dogs, some without, all smiling and happy to be there.

As Bridget surveyed the growing crowd in that courtyard, she thought back to the day she'd first moved in to this complex several months back. She'd had no clue what lay ahead.

That was the thing about moving.

You packed up your life into a series of boxes and prayed they would fit in well where you were going next.

Sometimes the pieces fit perfectly, but sometimes you needed new pieces—and that was totally okay.

"Are we ready?" Wesley asked, reaching for her hand. She'd asked him to lead their first walk together, and he'd easily settled into the role of coleader.

She laced her fingers through his. "Ready."

And she was. Ready to walk, ready to make new friends, ready for whatever came next.

Even though their relationship was still new and even though the sun still hung high in the early evening sky, Bridget felt as if she were walking into the beautiful sunset of her happily ever after.

Life wasn't just what you made of it.

It was who you let inside to share it with you.

And Bridget had the best friends in the entire world.

Recipes

Amy's Gingerbread Treats for Dogs & Their Humans

Ingredients
3 cups flour
2 Tablespoons chopped ginger
¾ teaspoon cinnamon
½ teaspoon whole cloves

1 cup water
¼ cup canola oil
¾ cup molasses
2 Tablespoons honey

Directions
Preheat the oven to 325°F. Combine the flour, ginger, cinnamon, and cloves in a large mixing bowl. Mix well, then add the water, oil, molasses, and honey to the bowl and stir. Continue to stir until the batter is thick but pliable. If needed, add flour to thicken or water to thin.

Transfer the dough to a cutting board and use cookie cutters to create cute shapes. I recommend creating gingerbread men, women, and canines!

Place the shapes on a greased baking sheet and bake them for 20 minutes. Remove the sheet from the oven and flip the cookies, then return them to the oven for 20 minutes.

Now you just have to wait for them to cool, decorate for the humans, leave plain for the dogs (or add a nice, tasty coating of peanut butter), and enjoy!

Wesley's (Not Bridget's) *Aloo Matar*

Ingredients
2 Tablespoons clarified butter (ghee)
Coriander, to taste
Cumin seeds, to taste
1 large white or yellow onion, chopped
2-3 garlic cloves, chopped
1-2 chopped fresh green chilis
2 teaspoons grated ginger
Ground mustard seed, to taste
Garam masala, to taste
Turmeric, to taste
Red chili powder, to taste
Salt, to taste
3 medium Roma tomatoes, chopped
2 large Idaho potatoes, peeled and cubed
½ cup freshly shelled peas
2 cups water
Whole-wheat pita bread (optional)
Basmati rice (optional)
Fresh cilantro (optional)

Directions
Place a large frying pan on medium heat and add the clarified butter. After the butter melts, add the coriander and cumin seeds followed by the onion, garlic, green chili, and ginger. Stir with a wooden spoon until the onion begins to brown. Mix in the ground mustard seed, garam masala, turmeric, and red chili powder to taste. Red chili and garam masala will make your dish spicy, so use sparingly unless you like it hot. Don't forget to add the salt!

Stir until the spices are blended into the mix. Add the

tomatoes and cook down to a thick stew-like consistency. Add the potatoes, peas, and water. Stir again.

Cover the pan with a lid until enough water evaporates to leave the desired thickness for your curry. Test a potato piece with a knife to ensure that the potatoes are tender.

Let the curry sit for at least fifteen minutes before serving with whole-wheat pita bread, basmati rice, or both. Consider adding fresh cilantro as a garnish. Enjoy!

ACKNOWLEDGMENTS

Wow, so many people to thank with this one. *Wednesday Walks & Wags* is the most difficult book I've ever written. Why? Because I handle anxiety and sorrow in the exact same way Bridget does.

Even though my mother is still alive and well (and has never had cancer a day in her life), writing Bridget's struggles meant writing out my own struggles.

The need to achieve, excel, keep busy no matter what—that's my everyday life. Like Bridget, I've always found a special kinship with animals. My very best friends as I grew up were a Calico cat named Pepsi and my ridiculously large collection of *The Baby-Sitters Club* books. I was a lonely kid without a fantastic friend group like the Sunday Potluck Club to see me through growing up and finding myself.

How lucky Bridget is to have that strong female support system!

These days, I have many friends and loved ones who care a great deal about me, but I still harbor that need to achieve in order to break through my troubles and come out ahead of life's many stressors.

I've been blessed to develop a support network that extends far beyond any one group or setting, and they are the ones who made this book possible even when a major depressive episode followed by a major health scare of my own made facing Bridget's trauma almost unbearable.

First, I must thank my eternally kind and understanding editor, Alicia Condon, and—indeed—the entire Kensington publishing team (Vida, Alex!). They believe in me even when

I'm not quite there myself. They saw something special in my words, in these characters, and they've truly made my dreams come true in a whole new way.

To my family and especially my husband, Falcon; my brother Ron; and my daughter, Phoenix. She may be just six, but she is definitely my biggest cheerleader with her never-ending stream of "C'mon, Mom, you can do it!"; "You're the very best author in the whole world, yes, you are!"; and my personal favorite, "Be strong and believe in yourself!"

Five of my six dogs and my one long-suffering cat deserve a huge thanks on this one. So, too, does the brand-new rescue kitty we adopted after I wrote Brownie's death—our daughter named him Merlin the Magical Fluff, and it's stuck.

All eight of my fur babies give me the cuddles and unwavering love that a woman just needs sometimes. My favorite Chihuahua girl, Sky Princess, even accompanied me when I locked myself in a hotel room for a week in a desperate bid to get those words written.

Of course, I'd also like to *not* thank my husky mix, Sitka, without whom this book would have been much easier to write. Funny, since I based Wesley's two dogs on her. Unfortunately, she had a spike in her anxiety that resulted in many barking, sleepless nights for our family. She is being treated now, and things are getting better. Thank goodness!

Thank you to Mallory, Angi, and Becky—my most constant supporters and friends. My family in Alaska, a big source of inspiration for this series.

My readers, friends, and well-wishers far and wide. Thank you for being there just when I needed you. Thank you for taking this journey with me. Thank you for being wonderful you!

WEDNESDAY WALKS & WAGS

Melissa Storm

ABOUT THIS GUIDE

The suggested questions are included to enhance your group's reading of Melissa Storm's *Wednesday Walks & Wags*.

DISCUSSION QUESTIONS

1. The story begins with Bridget avoiding opening her late mother's box. The same box reappears at several points in the story—after she learns about Wesley's time in prison and again in the final chapters. Each time the box appears, how do Bridget's reactions reflect her current emotional state and psychological journey?

2. How does the loss of her mother inform Bridget's choices throughout the novel? Do you think Bridget would have reacted differently to the events in her life if her mother hadn't died? Would there still be a story at all?

3. Bridget is afraid to veer off the path she set for herself because she worries her mother won't recognize her from Heaven. Do you think our loved ones look down on us after they're gone? Why is this idea both comforting *and* frightening for Bridget?

4. Bridget's mother leaves her a bucket list with items that include eating at a Michelin-starred restaurant, counting the stars, and falling in love. If you had a bucket list, what might it include? Do you think Bridget and Wesley will ever complete the list? Why or why not?

5. No matter what's going on in their lives, the members of the Sunday Potluck Club still meet every week. How does each character handle Bridget's grief differently? Who helps Bridget the most, and how?

6. What do food and cooking represent in this novel? Consider the friends' weekly potlucks, Bridget's ice-cream addiction, Wesley's job as a short-order cook, and the Indian food they prepare together before she introduces him to her friends.

7. Why does Bridget continue to meet Wesley in the courtyard despite his initial rudeness? Does he offer something she can't find from her friends? If so, what?

8. How are Bridget and Wesley's journeys similar, and what are their key differences?

9. Why did Wesley avoid telling Bridget about his past? Were his actions understandable, both in deciding to hide the truth and in choosing not to acknowledge it when Trent forced a confrontation at the Potluck Club?

10. What role do the animals in this story play? Particularly Teddy, Bridget's Pomeranian?

11. Discuss the significance of the plush toy Wesley gives to Bridget, which she later gives back to him. Is it important that the toy looks like Bridget's dog Teddy? Does it represent something larger than a simple gift?

12. What draws Wesley to Bridget, and at what point does he begin to care about her?

13. Dr. Kate warns Bridget that her big heart will make a career as a veterinarian difficult but later decides it is an asset. Why the shift in her opinion? Which do you think is true? Would Bridget make a good veterinarian? Why was she so committed to that path despite her obvious passion for volunteering at the shelter?

14. What do you think of Wesley's history with his friend Jon? How did both the betrayal and his time in prison shape his character? What would you have done in his position? And would you have chosen to keep the truth from Bridget? Do you believe his story when he finally shares it?

15. Should Bridget have forgiven Wesley? Do you think he'll be open with her now? Will their relationship last?

16. What does running represent in the story? How is it important to both Bridget and Wesley? How does it bring them together? Drive them apart?

17. Hazel and Keith have all orange flowers at their wedding to contrast with the white flowers at her father's funeral, which was held at the same church. What is the significance of having both events at the same place? How are weddings and funerals alike?

18. How do the scenes with Bridget's father and brother contribute to Bridget's overall character growth?

19. Throughout the novel, Bridget reflects on how to live a good life. Were there any particular thoughts or passages that stuck with you? Which ones?

20. What is the significance of the title *Wednesday Walks & Wags*? What other titles might have been a good fit for Bridget's journey?

Manic Monday, INC.

Nichole Peterson believes in rules, routines, and checklists—even more so after almost losing her father to cancer two years ago. Now she lives in constant fear of saying the wrong thing, knowing any conversation could be their last.

She met her best friends at the hospital right before each of them lost a parent, and as the only member of the Sunday Potluck Club with a surviving patient, she has a hard time opening up to them about the struggles that come with remission, with the fear of knowing the cancer could always come back and destroy everything.

When her primary care physician retires, the new partner who takes his place diagnoses her with obsessive-compulsive disorder, a condition she refuses to accept. As the weeks pass, though, it becomes more and more clear that her rituals and routines are no longer enough to keep her fear under control. A blowup at work forces her to take an extended leave, throwing her entire schedule off-balance.

But she can't talk to her father, can't talk to her friends . . . It seems the only person she can confide in these days is her best friend's big brother, Caleb.

Unlike Nichole, Caleb lives his life completely carefree and devoid of any structure. He never got a job, never left home, and yet this struggling novelist is the happiest person she's ever met. How? And can he help her find the self she hid so far away she can scarcely remember who she once was? Can these two unlikely allies discover full, balanced lives together? And maybe even find something extra special along the way?

Please turn the page for a preview of Melissa Storm's next book, *Manic Monday, Inc.*, coming soon from Kensington Publishing.

Nichole Peterson never went anywhere without her notebook. She used it to keep her schedule, draft lists, and to jot down reminders for later. Everyone teased her about her reliance on pen and paper when the whole world had gone digital now, but the heft of the notebook and the smell of the ink from her favorite ballpoint pen gave her comfort—security—in a way that a mishmash of apps never could.

She knew this because she'd tried more than once. She'd even switched over to the more modern method for a few years after college.

But then her father had gotten sick. . . .

For almost an entire year, she'd escorted him to doctor's appointments, stayed at his side for hospital stays, and turned to her notebook for direction.

People always liked to say that once something made its way onto the Internet, it would stay there forever. Perhaps that's why she'd superstitiously refused to keep the important details of his health on a device that was always connected to the web. Her mind made up, the notebook made its grand return and became more important than ever before.

Crazily enough, Nichole's plan somehow worked.

Her father's prostate cancer went into remission, and they both got on with their lives as if those horrible months of wondering, waiting, praying had been nothing more than a tiny blip on the radar.

Well, at least her father got on with his life. He found a new joy in all the little motions of day-to-day living that he'd once rushed through without taking the time needed to fully appreciate them—cooking, exercise, work, even just driving around the neighborhood. She loved how happy he was, now that he'd grabbed onto his second chance with both hands. . . .

But Nichole just didn't feel the same way.

She couldn't focus on the miracle of his recovery, because that meant accepting and moving past the devastation of his diagnosis—and that, she just could not do. Because now she'd learned the truth, that her world could all be taken away at any moment with hardly any notice.

Jotting it all down in her notebook, though, gave a bit of permanence to the capriciousness of life. If she could capture a thought, a need, a plan, she could control it—and if she could control it, then she didn't feel lost. At least not quite as much.

Even so, she constantly worried that the cancer would return and take her father from her once and for all. Each day was a gift, but it was also one day closer to the time he would eventually leave her. Whether it was cancer or something else, eventually he'd go.

Knowing that terrified her.

Especially since the very same thing had happened to her friend Bridget. Her mother had no sooner celebrated five years in remission than the family got the news that it was time to restart the clock, that the cancer had come back, ready to succeed where it had failed the last time around.

Less than six months later, Bridget's mom was dead.

Dutifully, Nichole went to the funeral and the bizarre after-party her friend had insisted on throwing afterward. She'd also gone to the funeral for Hazel's father and Amy's mother.

As much as cancer had taken from all of them, it had also given them something undeniably important. *One another.*

Nichole still remembered kind, motherly Amy introducing herself in the hospital cafeteria. She'd brought homemade cookies and offered to share. After that, they timed their coffee breaks together and eventually their parents' appointments, too.

A couple months later, they met Bridget, the youngest one in their group. When Hazel joined them, they decided to move their meetings offsite—not just because Hazel's father decided to refuse treatment, thus cutting her off from the hospital and the rest of the group, but also because they all needed an escape from the sterile landscape of their lives.

And so the Sunday Potluck Club was born. Every Sunday, they each brought a dish to pass and problems to share. Although the others considered Nichole the hard, cynical one, she found them to be her lifeline when navigating her fears and exploring her grief.

That was, until each of her friends lost a parent while Nichole's dad got better. Now the thing that held them together no longer included Nichole. If her friends were jealous, they did a good job hiding it. And she doubted they were, really.

No, *Nichole* was the problem. Not them.

Every time she looked at any of them, she was reminded of just how unfair—just how uneven—life could be. Why had her parent been saved? And how much longer would he be safe from the vile disease that had already taken so much?

She couldn't confide these troubles to her friends, so she sometimes wrote them in her notebook instead. Nobody would feel sorry for her, and she didn't want them to. But she also didn't expect them to understand her special form of suffering, of uncertainty.

The greatest irony of all, though, was that Nichole helped others heal every single day of the week in her work as a counselor. She specialized in helping military families and veterans as a social worker, which meant she dealt with a lot of post-traumatic stress.

And here she was battling the same symptoms because of the stress of a trauma that had never actually happened. Her father had lived. She needed to snap out of it, even though she'd never say such a thing to one of her charges.

When she was in college, everyone liked to say that people chose to pursue careers in psychology, social work, or other forms of counseling because they themselves were damaged. Nichole chose that work out of a fascination with both the human mind and how various socioeconomic factors could shape the outcome of a person's life. Her education had been an intellectual pursuit, not a journey of self-discovery. She'd never considered herself "messed up" or damaged.

Until her father's cancer had changed everything.

Now she had a wealth of knowledge on how to guide others to recovery, but still she couldn't find a way to help herself. And she was beginning to think nobody could help her, though she was willing to give it one last try.

She took a deep breath and pushed open the door to Dr. Anderson's office. Maybe she would have the answers Nichole had failed to find. If nothing else, she could cross one more thing off her list.